The Ghost Duke Who Loved Me

Cynthia Hunt

Copyright © 2023 Cynthia Hunt

All rights reserved.

To my parents, who showed me what a good love story looks like.

The Journey

An Ancient Wood, Yorkshire, 1806
  Midnight

It is a truth well-acknowledged that a young woman alone in the middle of a dark forest in the dead of night fleeing from almost certain death would rather be anywhere else.

That is, unless that woman was Miss Lisette Georgiana Havens, and the night in question was this one.

For Lisette, the current circumstances were, all things considered, a marked improvement. Her unknown future in this godforsaken forest, half-frozen and penniless, was far brighter than the one she faced if her pursuers caught up with her, or, even worse, she became the Marchioness of Ulster. She had no doubts about that.

Pulling her threadbare cloak around her shoulders, Lisette dodged and ducked, avoiding low hanging branches and any rocks big enough to be visible through the thick fog, and reflected on the events that led her to this moment.

The letter had arrived one week ago. Her uncle had dropped it unceremoniously on her desk, narrowly missing the chipped ink pot already there. Lisette had been in the middle of penning a missive to her only friend, Jemima. Jem had married a year ago and moved to Devon, but their lifelong friendship was just as strong as ever. Jem's husband was a sea captain, off to serve king and country nearly as soon as they wed, leaving Jem alone in a very quaint seaside cottage. She had a lot of time to write.

So did Lisette.

The chickens are recovering nicely after the freeze. Penny's wing is still hurting her, but she improves every day, thank you for ask-

The envelope landed with a thunk.

"Good god!" Lisette exclaimed, righting the ink pot and picking up the letter that had unsettled it. "What is this?"

"Read it. Aloud." As always her uncle left her no choice. "And watch your language."

A knot of dread pooled in Lisette's stomach. This was more attention than her uncle had paid her in a fortnight, and they were the only two in the house, besides the cook.

She opened the envelope and unfolded the thin parchment inside. A faint, spidery hand she did not recognize had scrawled carelessly across the page. Clearing her throat, she read aloud:

My Dear Mr. Pembroke,

It pleases me immeasurably that we should be in accord on this matter. I accept your proposal, or rather, I acknowledge that you accept mine. Deliver your niece ten days hence at Gosden Hall. I shall procure the license.

Apollo's Fire shall be sent over forthwith.

Sincerely,
Ulster

"What is this?"

Lisette's uncle, Nigel Pembroke, was a man of few words. Those he did utter were often cold and cruel. The words he spoke now were no different. "It's business, Lisette. Don't ask stupid questions. Have your things packed by morning. I've already asked Mrs. Fulsham to accompany you as I will not have the time."

"Accompany me? Where am I going?"

Her uncle was halfway to the door. He barely looked back at her. "Don't bore me, girl. Read the damn letter."

"I did read the "damn letter" and I have never heard of this Gosden Hall, dear uncle," Lisette said boldly, knowing he hated it when she used unladylike language but that he would not stop her if she were quoting his own words back to himself. Besides, she was beginning to suspect she was upset. "Nor do I know why Ulster is involved, or what in heaven's name the flames of Jupiter has to do with it."

Her uncle, resenting the prolonged contact with his ward, turned fully to face her from the doorway. He sighed heavily. "Gosden Hall is your new home. It's in Yorkshire. Ulster refers to the Marquess of Ulster, your soon-to-be husband. He is venerable, respected, and unbelievably wealthy," her uncle recited these facts as thought reading a list of recipe ingredients, "and *Apollo's Fire*, my girl, is only the finest yearling in England. I should think you would have figured this out, you have always been too clever for your own good."

"I-" Lisette stammered, but he was already gone, the door shutting with a snap.

Lisette slumped in her chair, numb with shock. She was going to marry a man she had never met? She had barely even heard of him- and what she had, well, Ulster was certainly respected and wealthy, but he was also nearly eighty years old and renowned for his ill temper and battles with gout, if the gossip was correct. He had fathered nine daughters but never a son, despite at least four wives having assisted in the attempt. He had outlived them all. The wives, that is. She had no idea what had become of the daughters but surely some must be older than Lisette herself, perhaps much older, which would be dreadfully awk-

Her mind was rambling. This always happened when she was excited. Or curious. Or, in this case, deeply upset.

Lisette sighed and tried to quiet her racing thoughts. Sometimes she wished she was not clever at all. Wouldn't life be easier if she was as dumb and dull as the chickens in her yard? Dumber and duller, in truth. Even the chickens would have surely realized she was being sold, and her price was a race horse.

Lisette cried all that night, but by the next morning when old Mrs. Fulsham from the village had appeared to accompany her in the mail coach, there were no more tears to shed.

It was a cruel irony that Lisette had longed to travel her whole life, all twenty-one years of it, but her first real journey was also likely to be her last. Ulster, to her knowledge, never left Yorkshire, and certainly no wife of his would, either.

Lisette clambered into the mail coach feeling very much like she imagined Henry VIII's wives must have felt approaching the executioner. Pity her own demise would not be swift, nor her mode of reaching it so royal. The mail coach was hardly the glamorous equipage of her long-held travel fantasies. It was smelly and cramped. She and Mrs. Fulsham shared it with a pregnant young woman and her two restless children, an elderly farmer who reeked of beets, and a businessman whose girth took up enough space for two.

Even worse, every leg of the trip seemed to take forever. Lisette swore every bump in the road was magnified tenfold in the creaking old coach, but from her middle seat she could not look out the curtained window to confirm this theory.

"How far is Gosden Hall?" Lisette had asked Mrs. Fulsham after a particularly bone-rattling jostle.

"What was that?" the old woman had asked loudly. Lisette remembered she was hard of hearing.

"How far is Gosden Hall?" she shouted.

"Three days," the businessman had interjected from across the carriage. "In good weather. Now keep your voice down, young woman."

Three days? She could not possibly survive this for three days. Nor, she had thought with a queasy feeling unrelated to the motion of the coach, what came after.

But then, what choice did she have? What choice had she ever had?

The next two days and nights were a slow drip of misery. Even Lisette's usually racing thoughts had gotten bored and left her alone, meaning she had barely any thoughts at all. She tried to read, but it made her feel ill. She tried to sleep, but she kept being pushed into the middle of the bench seat and her only option was to lean on Mrs. Fulsham, which she refused to do. The old woman smelled of cabbage. She was left mostly closing her eyes and escaping in fantasies of running away and living in a beautiful cottage by the sea, just like Jem.

Small but well-appointed, the cottage in her mind had a view of the ocean- that bit was blurry, as Lisette had never seen it, but she had read a great deal about it- and a large garden. Lisette could spend her days reading and growing roses. She loved roses. She wanted more than anything to cultivate the very best. A third of her luggage was books on horticulture, much to her uncle's disgust. Lisette did not care what he thought, he was a self-absorbed idiot. Anyway, surely the sea air would be ideal for cultivating the most beautiful, fragrant, and hearty of blooms? Dreams of salt air and luscious, soft, lip-red petals filled her mind.

Then the farmer would belch or an infant would cry and Lisette had to start the fantasy all over again. And again. And again.

The first night they stayed at an inn with excellent pudding and terrible beds. In contrast, the second night's inn had terrible stew and surprisingly comfortable beds. That this was the foremost memory of her first journey since she had come to live with her uncle, at the age of three which meant she had no recollection of it, did nothing to lighten

Lisette's ever darkening thoughts.

A storm passed through on that second night, making the roads difficult the next day and slowing the coach down significantly. Lisette could not decide if that was a blessing or a curse. She did not want to arrive at Gosden Hall at all, but since that was not an option, late would be the next best thing, would it not?

Then again, was delaying the inevitable any better?

Lisette turned her thoughts back to the cottage and a particular bush of canary yellow blooms.

At least on the third day there were fewer occupants on the coach, the weather seemingly chased off other travelers. In addition to Lisette and Mrs. Fulsham there was a middle-aged woman in expensive clothing whom Lisette suspected was a governess. The firm set of her jaw gave her away. Across from the ladies sat the beet farmer, their only constant companion, and a quiet, thin young man with beautiful blue eyes. He was rather handsome, Lisette thought, but then, she knew very little of men. Not real ones, anyway. Books were no substitute for the living thing.

In reality? She knew horseflesh, thanks to her uncle's obsession with racing, and she knew chickens. She could identify a promising speckled hen in a flash or a rose variety simply by its smell. But a promising young gentleman?

She hadn't the faintest idea how to identify one of those.

Or what to do with one if encountered.

She had never expected to marry, after all. A woman with no dowry, no parents, no formal education in anything, and too many freckles was hardly a catch. That her uncle, her only family and legal guardian, was a notorious gamester was the cherry on top of- of nothing. There was nothing, except a rotten cherry and a girl with too many thoughts and too many books jostling around in her head.

The young man across the carriage caught her eye and smiled.

She inhaled sharply in surprise and succeeded in inhaling some bit of fluff floating about the carriage and coughing for the next two minutes. She had avoided the man's gaze after that and willed her face to return to a shade that did not match her frustratingly red hair. She must look like a strawberry. A coughing, fidgety strawberry.

No wonder the old Marquess of Ulster was the only one who wanted her.

Lisette decided she had to improve her thoughts. Self-pity was both unbecoming and unhelpful.

Maybe it would not be so terrible being the Marchioness of Ulster? She would have money. And a grand house. And the Marquess was very old. No man lived forever. The stress of having so many daughters and being so disagreeable must have worn him down, and based purely on his very thin and weak penmanship alone Lisette suspected he was not in good health. Was penmanship a good way to judge someone's vitality?

Yes, Lisette decided. It must be. With any luck Ulster would die soon. Lisette did not usually wish death on people, but in this case, his all too timely demise would be her only chance at a bearable life and god help her, she was a selfish creature.

Yes, she thought in the now dark carriage- they were going so slowly they would need to stop for another night after all- being a young, moneyed widow with a title would not be the worst fate in the world.

A loud bang sounded outside and the horses screamed. Lisette jumped, half landing on Mrs. Fulsham.

"Pardon, girl," the old woman grumbled, having not heard the bang. "Watch yourself!"

The carriage slowed to a stop. There was shouting nearby, coming closer.

"What's this about?" the governess asked no one in particular and no one answered. Footsteps were drawing near.

Lisette heard the coachman above say "Here now, gents, nothing for you on this one I promise you. If you'd just-"

Another loud bang followed by a thud against the top of the carriage. Lisette's ever racing thoughts were coming to a terrible conclusion.

She was too frightened to scream.

"Why are you making that face, girl?" Mrs. Fulsham blinked at her, still oblivious to the fact that they were clearly being overtaken by highwaymen.

Lisette made a shushing gesture just as the governess reached out a hand to open the door opposite the sounds of the men outside.

"I wouldn't do that if I were you," a low voice said, clear as ice.

Lisette looked up and saw the young man with the beautiful eyes was holding a pistol. He pointed it first at the governess and then each of the other occupants in turn. When he got to Lisette, he held her gaze with a particularly cruel glint in his eye.

"You're a sorry lot," he said. He had not spoken all day and his voice was reedy and cruel. It made him instantly unattractive and Lisette was sorry for it. But then, there were greater concerns afoot.

There are other attractive men in the world and when you are a vibrant young widow, you can go to London, and meet them, and- Lisette caught herself. This was no time to let her thoughts get away from her. This was a time for- for-

For something useful. She knew highwaymen sometimes only took some valuables and left. She also knew sometimes they did far worse things, and based on the the fact these ones seemed to have already killed the driver, she suspected these were the latter, worse type.

"Alright, git out, evry'un," the young man said in thick accent she could not place, but then, she had never been anywhere before.

They all did as the young man directed, stumbling on travel-weakened legs to stand on the muddy road. A giant of a man was standing there holding a pistol in each hand with another, shorter man standing beside him. They heard a rustling sound and Lisette saw there was a fourth figure rummaging through their luggage behind the coach. The rear coachman slumped at his feet, but whether unconscious or worse, Lisette could not tell.

The night air was cold and a bitter breeze swept down from the north, promising bad weather. They were on the edge of a wood, which she supposed was where the highwaymen had been lying in wait. Looking at the others cowering beside her, Lisette stood tall. She, too, was terrified, but she did not like the look of cowardice and she, all things considered, had nothing to lose.

Whatever her fate was going to be, she might as well face it head held high.

The short man walked forward, his focus immediately on Lisette. Her bravery wavered, but she kept did not let it show.

"Well ain't this a pretty bit o'muslin, lads." The words were met with dark chuckling and something mumbled by the man at the rear of the carriage that Lisette was grateful she could not hear. It made the man who had gone to assist him laugh even more darkly.

"What's your name, gel?" the short man, who was the obviously the leader of the gang, asked her.

"Miss Havens," she said, proud of the strength of her voice.

"Oooh, Miss! She's gently bred, lads! Of course she is," he spoke, still addressing his comrades for effect. The other passengers stood, ignored and shivering, beside her.

"For now," said the young man who had ridden inside the carriage

and Lisette wondered how she ever found him handsome.

Her knees were trembling in earnest now, and it had nothing to do with the cold. She knew what these men intended, and she knew she had to find a way to escape them before they went through with it.

The short man was still walking towards her, slowly, appraisingly, and Lisette wracked her usually clever brain for an answer. There had to be a way out of this nightmare. There had to be some way she could escape. She was smarter than her uncle, and he swindled people all the time. He was always getting what he wanted and getting out of trouble. There must be some very ingenious solution, if only she could-

Some deep part of her mind spit out an answer then and realizing it was the best idea she had- the *only* idea she had- she went with it.

"Oh sirs! Please don't hurt me! I'm a lady!" she cried out, and raising a hand to her brow, she crumpled to the cold, muddy ground.

The highwaymen laughed in earnest this time. "Didn't even touch her, lads! This one is true quality!" the leader said gleefully, and Lisette wanted to kick him with her boots and knock him to the ground, too.

Instead, she remained motionless. After a moment a pair of rough hands scooped her up. It took every fiber of willpower she possessed to remain limp, but she knew it was the only chance her plan would work. Surely they had to deal with the others before they got around to whatever they wished to do with her.

Right?

Thankfully, her gamble paid off. She had been prepared to pull the small dagger she kept in her boot out if the man who had carried her to the side of the road had been untoward, but he had not. He had simply set her down in the wet grass at the edge of the forest, like a sack of grain he would worry about later.

This was even better than she had hoped for. She could not say luck was on her side, as she had just been waylaid by highwaymen and was in genuine mortal peril, but luck had not forsaken her entirely.

When the man who carried her returned to the group huddled by the carriage, Lisette peeked open one eye. The highwaymen, pistols out, were demanding the other passengers empty their pockets. Poor Mrs. Fulsham looked like she was going to genuinely faint.

That instinct from deep inside Lisette's mind chirped again and she knew it was now or never. The highwaymen would not leave her alone for long.

Grateful they had left her close to the darkly shadowed trees that marked the start of the forest, Lisette quietly rose. A sliver of the moon so fine it was barely visible in the night's shifting fog was the only illumination beyond the small circle of light the highwaymen's torches created. Everyone was focused there, on the passengers on their hoped-for riches. No one was looking her way, she just had to dash-

Something grabbed her arm, a hand pressing over her mouth.

"Not so fast, luvvy. You think we'd let a pretty little thing like you get away?"

The young man from the carriage was behind her. She should have counted the men before she moved. Fool!

Without thinking, she kicked up her heel, all her force directed between the man's legs.

He howled and fell to the ground.

"You bitch!" he cried, calling the other men's attention to them.

So Lisette did the only thing she could: she ran.

Gunshots rang out behind her, but she did not have time to consider whether they were meant for her. She was already in the line of trees. The forest was very old and there was little bracken covering the ground so she could run as fast as her skirts allowed.

It was not fast enough. She heard two of the highwaymen running behind her. Grateful for a childhood spent mostly ignored in the countryside, playing in fields and streams and younger forests to the south, she darted and ducked through the ancient trees.

It was an eery forest, dark and still. It would have sent a chill up her spine, if worse dangers, real dangers, were not close behind and catching up.

Ignoring a stitch in her side and a sudden, sharp pain in her right foot, Lisette urged herself to go faster.

A branch appeared from the darkness and her head smacked right into it. She tumbled to the ground, dazed. The footsteps were close now. Too close.

But she could not stop.

Rising unsteadily she turned away from the approaching footsteps and froze. She was standing in front of a gate, part of a tall stone wall that disappeared into the darkness as far as she could see, all as ancient and forgotten as the trees themselves. Without thinking, Lisette ran forward and gave the half rotten gate a push. It gave way just enough for her to squeeze through.

Unfortunately, it also creaked. Loudly.

"Over there!" one of the men called.

"On it!" another one said, much closer. "When I catch the little bitch I'm gonna-"

"Wait!" the first man called, having nearly caught up to the second. They were so close Lisette dared not run. She remained still and silent, curled into the shadowy vines at the base of the stone wall. It was so dark she did not think they would notice her even if they did pass through themselves.

As her pursuers only a few feet away on the other side of the gate, Lisette prayed to whatever powers watched over this forsaken place she was right. Her ankle was hurting like mad and she did not know how much further it would take her.

"What is it?" the second man said irritably. He was breathing heavily. "She's getting away!"

"Let 'er," the first one said grimly. "You know where we is don't ya? No good comes of no one as enters 'ere. I ain't afraid of no man as walks this earth but what's in there I won't cross."

The was a long pause, then the second man spoke. "Let it 'ave 'er, then. We'll find another bit o'fun." There was a a new note in his gruff voice. It sounded like fear.

Lisette did not move a muscle. She barely breathed. Then, just as quickly as they had ambushed the carriage, they men turned around and disappeared back into the night, eager to return to their comrades. Or, Lisette thought with a chill, to get away from whatever lived on this side of the wall.

As if on cue, a twig snapped nearby, and Lisette took off running again.

She ran several more minutes but heard nothing else. Nothing at all, actually. Somehow that was worse.

At least the trees were thinning. She wondered if perhaps there was a village nearby. A village that disliked outsiders. That would explain the men's trepidation, and while it was understandable a community might dislike men like the highwaymen, Lisette doubted anyone would turn away a helpless young woman with nothing on a night like this.

Even if there was no village, she had run so far there must be an inn or a country house or a farm or, or…. something. A cozy woodsmen's cottage with a blazing hearth, and a family, and maybe a large, woolly dog.

A clearing abruptly appeared. Lisette stepped right into it, the difference with the thick woods just a step behind like night and day. It was, however, still very much night. Clouds were covering the stars and that little sliver of moon was gone. Grateful for a little open air, Lisette paused to catch her breath. She tried hard to ignore the burning in her lungs and the worsening pain in her ankle. Instead, she turned her mind longingly to roasted ham and mulled wine and the happy company of a warm, woolly dog.

She was about to sit down, just for a moment, when the clouds parted. She turned about then, to see her surroundings.

It was not a clearing, as she had thought, a clearing. It was, or had been, a driveway. Overgrown and wild now, there were still flagstones underfoot, covered in moss and grass. It was these that had kept the ever spreading trees at bay.

Her gaze followed the flat lines of the roadway ahead, away from the wall of the forest, and met with… another wall entirely.

Lisette's breath hitched. It was a house.

The relief she had imagined did not come, however. The habitation before her was the farthest thing from a welcoming cottage she had ever seen. It was massive. It took up all her vision as she stood facing it, rising from the trees so high she could have sworn the topmost tower touched the clouds.

As her eyes traveled over the crumbling, ivy-covered stone walls, along the jagged roofline, she saw something hanging from the end of one jutting eave. The clouds shifted again and shone on the focus of her attention, which danced in the cold breeze. Lisette peered more closely, trying to make out just what it was- and then, she did something she had never done in all her life.

She screamed.

The Shelter

The object was not hanging, it was falling, plummeting straight at her. Lisette ducked as the enormous barn owl screeched a piercing cry and barely missed her. With a rush of massive wings it cried once more and disappeared into the trees behind her.

Shaken, she rose.

Silly nitwit, she chided herself. It was just an owl. Of course there would be barn owls in a place like this. There was nothing to fear. Rather, she should be grateful to find shelter for the night. The clouds were thickening above and it looked like rain was imminent. She was better off finding some place to curl up and hide for the night. The highwaymen knew which way she had gone, but it was obvious they had no desire to follow her here. Besides, the house was clearly massive and surely there was some spot she could conceal herself well enough that even if anyone came looking they would not find her.

Lisette took a fortifying breath and stepped forward.

There was barely enough light to see where she was going, but carefully Lisette approached the old house, if one could call such a massive pile a house, and looked for a door. There were a couple of broken windows, but she did not dare enter that way. The glass protruding from the sills was jagged and her ankle was already giving her enough pain.

A freezing wind whipped past her and moments later she felt the first droplets of rain. She needed to find a way in soon. If she got drenched out here in these temperatures she doubted even a big fire and a woolly dog could save her.

Like a bucket tipped over, the rain began in earnest. *Damn it*, Lisette thought. This was bad.

Then she saw it. Dim in the darkness, she could made out a heavy old oak door. A sudden crack and flash of lightning, startlingly bright, confirmed her suspicion. Praying again to whatever forces were listening tonight that the door was unlocked, she hurried over to it.

Slipping on the slick stones at her feet, she took the massive iron handle in hand and gave it a push.

Nothing happened.

Releasing a little huff of frustration Lisette tried again, pressing with all her might against the door.

Still nothing.

"Damn it," she hissed aloud this time. Like any well bred young lady she rarely cursed, but if there was a time for it, it was now. If only her uncle could hear her. *Damn him, too.*

The wind whirled with a howl, blowing leaves and rain against her skirts and the face of the house. The air sounded like it was laughing at her, which only increased her frustration- and her determination to open the door.

Stepping back, she decided to try once more with all her strength. If that failed, the broken windows would have to do.

Leaning forward with her shoulder poised for contact, Lisette ran at the door as fast as the slick stones underfoot would allow.

With a crack of old wood and a thick thud, the door opened- before she reached it.

Alarmed, it was too late to pull back and she hurtled full force through the doorway and straight into a large upholstered wooden chair.

She slid to the floor, leaning against the chair in a cloud of dust so thick she could barely breathe. Coughing, she could not protest when the impossibly heavy door she had just passed through shut behind her.

It took a moment for the very literal dust to settle. She sat in the darkness, catching her breath and gathering her thoughts. She was inside, that was good. She was out of the rain, that was good. It was nearly pitch black inside, which was not ideal but as the place seemed deserted, was not the worst outcome. The door had opened and shut itself, which was curious and alarming, but given the wind, not surprising, surely. The door was impossibly heavy but then the wind was howling now.

Lisette may be out of the rain but as she turned her attention to her person, she realized she was very wet already and very, very cold. *That* was bad and had to take the highest priority. She needed a fire as soon as possible or she would not last the night.

Rising shakily she stood and continued her self-assessment. Her ankle was still painful, but it was also increasingly numb. That was probably bad but felt better. She was certain she looked a fright, but as there was no one around to care, she did not, either. Everything else seemed in working order.

Next, Lisette took in her surroundings, which were becoming clearer as more dust settled and her eyes adjusted to the almost nonexistent light. There was another sharp crack and explosion of lightning outside, destroying her progress but giving her a few moments of full illumination inside the house.

It was undeniably a house, not some forgotten inn, and a very old house at that. The furnishings were coated in dust and grime and shabby, but obviously well-made. Everything she saw spoke to long distant money and the expensive tastes of a bygone era. While the styles may be out of date, the quality was not. Even the chair she had fallen into had barely registered her sudden assault. It was sturdy, with thick legs carved into the most ornate and unnecessary design of dragons twining around them.

Lisette wondered why the house was abandoned, and, as it obviously had been neglected for some time, why no ne'er-do-wells had absconded with all the finery inside. Everything looked untouched, as if one day the home's occupants had simply walked out and never returned.

The lightning flashed again, confirming her first impression. As everything was plunged back into utter darkness, Lisette remained still, her mind racing to complete her mental inventory.

She had shelter, that was good. The place seemed utterly deserted, which was not as good as finding a welcoming family of well-provisioned woodsmen and that hypothetical woolly dog, but was certainly better than stumbling into a hideout filled with hostile bandits.

The roof seemed solid and everything inside was very dry. A positive.

She, still, was not. Negative.

Despite no experience navigating real life-threatening situations Lisette had lived long enough and read widely enough to know she needed to get dry and warm as soon as possible.

She shut her eyes and counted to ten.

When she opened them again she could see a little better. Not by much, but it was enough to make out the shapes of the big pieces of furniture, the outline of a large staircase rising out of the back of the entry hall, and some darker areas on the walls she guessed were doors.

She guessed correctly, at least with the door she chose. It was the nearest to the front door and she hoped the room it concealed held a workable fireplace.

Lisette took the door handle and pushed. Nothing.

She pushed harder. Still nothing. Finally she pushed with all her might, and despite her considerable exhaustion there was an almighty groan of the old wood. Unfortunately, that was it.

"*Pull...*" a voice hissed, low and deep and right behind her.

She spun around in the dark.

She was alone.

There was no one there. No one and nothing at all. The hairs on her neck rose.

Grateful she did not believe in spirits, Lisette decided this was no time to start.

She turned back to the door and further decided that it must have been her own instincts telling her to pull on the door handle. It was obvious, really. There were only two ways to open a door and she had already tried one.

She grasped the door handle and, calling once more on all her strength, she pulled.

The ancient door opened easily. So easily, Lisette toppled over backwards and crashed to the floor as another flash of lightning and thunder cascaded over the house.

In the sudden light she could see what lay behind the now open door.

It was a storage closet.

"*Run,*" the same voice as before said, even closer now.

Lisette froze, a chill unrelated to any night air running through her. Her instincts screamed at her, telling her to heed the voice. She should leave. Now. There was a darkness in this place, some ephemeral danger. The highwaymen had been right to turn around.

She rose unsteadily to her feet, so cold it was impossible to move with any grace. Her hands were shaking from more than just the chill.

"GO," the voice roared all around her at the same time she heard the unmistakable sound of a window shattering up above.

Glass fell with a hideous sound all around her, barely missing her person.

"GET OUT," the voice shouted again, as much a howling wind as a voice, its anger palpable all the same. *"AGHHHH!"*

With a tremendous scream the voice or the wind or whatever it was blasted through her like ice, a deadly cold force moving straight to the door. It forced her back a step in that direction, but widened her stance to steady herself.

She should be running. She should be *screaming* and running. Surely taking her chances in the woods in the approaching storm was better than whatever devilry was afoot inside this rightfully forgotten house?

The wind inside reached the front door and opened it, pulling it inwards with an almighty bang as the thick wood crashed into the wall. Rainy wind came streaming in, casting leaves and twigs and bits of house around the floor, just as Lisette felt the wind inside the house behind her again, pushing her to leave.

She turned around.

Nothing. There was nothing there. She felt the wind, but it was not strong enough to make her move if she stood against it.

"RUN FOR YOUR LIFE GIRL," the voice roared around her, another crash above sending more debris down to the floor a few feet away from her. This time it appeared to be the better part of an old cabinet. *"LEAVE THIS PLACE. ONLY DEATH AWAITS YOU HERE."*

Lisette took one step towards the open door, rain streaming in now from the forest outside. Then she took another, then another.

"GOOD GIRL," the voice in the wind hissed and she swore she could feel its breath on her neck, like a lover's words, but cold as death.

She stopped.

This all reminded her of something.

It was an admittedly strange time to be reflective, given that she should be running for her life from the most terrifying and bizarre phenomenon she had ever encountered, but there was something off about the whole thing, if only she could put her finger on it.

Oh, her mind was screaming at her to run, far louder than

any mysterious voice. She certainly did not wish to die tonight. Very old, in bed, with a hot water bottle and some grandchildren asleep in another room? Those were the circumstances she wished for when she finally moved on to whatever other realm awaited her.

No, Lisette did not wish to die, but some deeper instinct within her told her she would not die in this place. There was more here than there appeared to be and this voice, whatever it was, was not what it seemed.

The voice *reminded* her of something. Or, more precisely, someone.

"LEEAAVVEEEEE," the voice screamed again, raging around her like a child having a tantrum.

"That's it!" she exclaimed, triumphant.

The wind quieted slightly, as if to hear her better. Perhaps in the cold she had lost her mind and she was in truth passed out in some ditch in the woods dreaming, but she did not think that was the case. This was real. The wind was here and it was listening.

The cold would overcome her though if she did not find warmth, and soon. She needed a fire.

Her mind raced to piece her tangled thoughts together.

"Yes, I've got it!"

The wind- and she did not think wind could do this- paused. Just stopped. The house was silent just like that, with only the sounds of the storm outside continuing on.

"What… have you…. *got?*" the voice asked. It was not screaming any longer. It was creaking and broken, like the sound of dry leaves. It came from all around her, and sounded like it was out of practice saying anything more than "get out" and "leave."

"You remind me of someone," Lisette, who had never conversed with a house before, said simply. "I just remembered who. It's obvious, really. I don't know why it took me so long."

There was a long pause, during which the rain and wind outside continued violently, dashing more bits of forest debris in through the still open front door. Another flash of lightning and accompanying thunder illuminated the scene. It looked like the storm had hit inside as much as out, but in a way, Lisette supposed it had. The house looked terrible.

And yet, it seemed to have some vanity, because after what seemed like an age, it hissed thoughtfully, "whooooo?"

"My uncle Nigel."

The house, presumably having never met Uncle Nigel, had nothing to say to that, and so it simply waited for her to continue.

Ignoring the fact that she was now fully conversing with an abandoned mansion, Lisette obliged. "He is my father's younger brother. He is a businessman of sorts, but really he just swindles people and gambles. He's not very good at it, but he thinks the world of himself. He demands complete obedience despite earning absolutely no respect from anyone in the household. He is unmarried, unkind, and unreasonable. When he does not get his way he stomps and yells and carries on until someone gives in, usually out of pity, or until he is exhausted, or drunk. Usually drunk. He is, in short, a child."

The house had remained silent and still for the entirety of her speech. There was a beat as it took in her words, and then,

"GETTT OUTTTTT," it howled louder than ever before, a wind like a tempest violently whirling around the hall and she could hear it banging about the upper stories, too. Now all manner of bits of wood and pebbles and tapestry were falling down from the stories above into the open space of the grand staircase and onto the entryway floor.

This only confirmed Lisette's suspicions, and her conviction.

"You are a bully," she said loud and firm. She knew the house could hear her, even as it whipped her words away and they were lost in the mayhem.

She turned back to the right side of the hall and made for the second door. There were never two storage closets side by side. The next door in line had to be a proper room.

She pulled on the door first, but it was obvious this one did not work that way. It was a strangely designed house, she thought, but then, perhaps that was part of why it was so very vain. She would be frightfully self-conscious if I were in this state and probably just as ill-tempered.

The wind growing behind her, and with a crash something shattered against the wall to her right. She did not look to see what it was, but knew she had to act quickly. If the house had decided to start throwing things at her it was only a matter of time before she was bludgeoned with an old cabinet or impaled by a dead tree branch.

"I SAID GET OUT!" the wind screeched in a deafening explosion all around her. Leaves and her own hair, long undone, lashed at Lisette's face, but she knew if she could get to the other side of this door, she stood a chance. The house needed to understand that she was not leaving tonight.

"I'm staying!" she shouted back and pushed the door with all her might.

The Welcome

There was a dreadful pause, then the door gave way with an angry creak of its ancient hinges.

Lisette pulled herself inside, fighting the wind, which now seemed to be trying to drag her away. As she entered the room beyond the door she pushed it back against the wind until, with a shudder, it snapped shut. A large brass key was resting in the lock on this side. Lisette turned it.

The moment she did, she leaned against the door for support, breathing hard. Her hair and skirts settled back into place, albeit a very unkempt one. There was no wind in here, and though it was irrational, she sensed there would not be, now that she had locked the door. She would not be chased away so easily.

She took a deep, exhausted breath and released a heavy sigh.

The smells of dust and mildew hit her first, followed by the undeniable scent of smoke. She grinned. There was a fireplace in here.

Turning to face the still, dark space, she tried to make out what sort of room she was in.

It was a little easier to see in this room than the dour entryway. This space was large. It had a high ceiling and a row of windows along one long wall. The walls and ceiling were paneled in dark oak in an antique style, but then, everything about this place was old.

The floor creaked as Lisette stepped forward and she jumped, the wind whipping up outside and pelting rain against the windows. It still sounded like laughter.

The sounds from the hall had stopped. The house was

quiet. Lisette shuddered. Its silence was more unsettling than its anger. She knew it was watching her, waiting.

Lisette took a deep breath to steady herself. It was difficult, as she was freezing, but the hope of some warmth was nearer than before. She continued deeper into the room.

She knew her target. Taller than she was, and twice as wide as its height, a black hollow in one wall beckoned. Lisette smiled. The dark cavern of an inglenook fireplace was unmistakeable. She made for it, her sense of the space improving with every step forward.

A flash of lightning confirmed her suspicions. It was a fireplace larger than her chicken coop back home. She had never seen anything so beautiful.

"But how to start the fire?" she mumbled to herself.

"The flint's on the mantle," a new voice, dry and sardonic, said right behind her.

Lisette jumped just as the lightning flashed again, this time with a riotous crash of thunder right on top of the house. She spun around. No one was there.

Of course.

"So helpful," she replied sardonically. "But I would rather not take your advice, given the my gracious welcome in the hall."

"Suit yourself," this new voice said, a little farther off now.

She waited a few moments until there was another flash, then her eyes rapidly scanned the floor along the grate. There was wood against the seat to the left, covered in cobwebs but obviously dry. Unfortunately it was useless if she did not have a way to light it.

Lisette bent down and began feeling along the edge of the wood pile. Nothing. Then she moved to the base of the fire grate. Nothing there, either. There had to be *something* here that would help, everything else had obviously been left in a hurry, in the middle of use, so why would-

"Good god, woman. The flint is on the bloody mantle, top right ledge," the new voice, now exasperated and undeniably male, said from the direction of the settee behind her.

"I may be freezing," Lisette stammered, shivering, "but I am not mad."

The voice mumbled something that sounded a lot like "women" just as another crack of lightning flashed. Thunder crashed like an explosion around the house, and Lisette decided that perhaps she, like the saints of old, was channeling perfectly reasonable divine advice. Absurd, yes- but what else had the tales of all those saints taught her if not to believe in the absurd?

Maybe all those Sundays her hypocritical uncle had dragged her to services would pay off after all. Maybe this voice did not belong to the house. Perhaps it was a guardian angel of some sort, in which case, perhaps there *was* flint on the mantle...

She stumbled upward, her feet and hands numb. She reached high, feeling along the little ledge at the right side of the mantle.

There was nothing there.

"There's nothing there," she said aloud, "serves me right, stupid house, playing tricks-"

"Apologies. I meant the *left* side."

Lisette straightened. "Oh, I am sure you did. And once I look there you'll assure me you meant the cabinet over there, and then it will be the little side table near the window- I am sure you must be bored to death but I will not be your plaything."

"Do not mock death," the voice said with an angry edge. A little breeze swept across the room in warning.

Lisette pursed her lips. "I do not like being threatened, sir, or, or whatever you are."

"You're not being threatened, you nitwit, you're wasting bloody time is what you're doing. *Left side.*"

Lisette gave an exasperated sigh that turned into a cough as she caught a mouthful of dust kicked up by the sudden breeze. This was nonsense. A fire, some sleep, and it would all prove to be a hallucinatory dream brought on by exposure.

She reached up to the little ledge on the left.

Her fingers were so numb it was difficult to tell what was there, but after a moment she heard the undeniable thwack of a small object hitting the floor. She had knocked something off.

"There you go," the voice said in a condescending tone. The voice was definitely male, and increasingly, Lisette suspected, well-moneyed. She had never met a pauper who could precisely capture that exact air of presumption and baseless arrogance.

"Are you the same voice that was in the hall?" she asked.

"How many spirits do you think live in this ruddy pile?"

She bent down to retrieve the fallen object. Her quarry in hand, she quickly straightened. "I haven't the faintest idea. I don't know anything about spirits."

"Good. I highly recommend keeping it that way," said the voice, dry and sardonic as ever. The angry child from before had been replaced by an arrogant, obviously bored man.

Lisette could tell from the feel and weight of the object in her hand that it was, indeed, flint. She looked around the room.

"Why are you helping me? I thought you wanted me to leave?"

"Oh, believe me, I do," the voice replied emphatically. "I simply realized you're braver than the others and therefore marginally more interesting."

"There have been others?" she asked, curious what had happened to anyone else who dared enter this awful house.

The voice continued, ignoring her. "You see, it occurred to me, when my usual persuasions failed to persuade you, that if you truly refuse to leave, I must, against my better judgment I might add, ensure you survive the night."

A chill that had nothing to do with the temperature went through Lisette. "Why is that?"

"Because if you die here, there will be two of us, and while I may already be in purgatory, that sounds like hell."

Her brow furrowed. "You're- a ghost?"

"Make the fire, girl. You're already chilled to the bone."

Though curiosity was gnawing at her, Lisette agreed with the voice. Or, rather, the ghost. The numbness was moving from her hands and feet deeper and deeper into her very marrow. She did not have much time.

She bent down beside the grate and assembled the wood. There was an old book on a table next to the other settee. She loved books, but surviving the night was more important, and the pages were dry. She ripped some out and crinkled them up with the logs. Finally, she struck the flint. It took a few tries, but soon a little flame danced merrily before her.

She nearly wept.

"Let me assist you," the ghost voice said, and a gentle breeze, like a heavy sigh wafted past her and the flames roared into life.

Lisette really did cry then. Just a little. She was going to be okay.

"Not so fast, soldier," the voice said, shifting behind her as if pacing. "Those rags you're passing off as clothing are drenched.

Fire's no good if you don't take them off."

Lisette blinked. "Excuse me?"

"There are blankets in the cabinet over there, to the left. They're dusty but not as moth-eaten as most of the others. It's a solid cabinet. Gift from Henry VII, I believe. Beautiful craftsmanship."

More thoughts flooded Lisette's mind, but the one that passed her lips was, "I can't undress in front of you."

The ghostly voiced laughed then, long and hard. It sounded odd though, creaking and dusty, as if it had not been used for such a purpose in a very long time.

Lisette scowled into the fire, having nowhere else to look. Finally, the laughter subsided.

"I don't see what's so funny. I'm a lady."

"You're a lady and I'm aether, so what does it matter? I'm hardly going to ravish you. I haven't had a body in nearly a century."

Lisette knew the aether had a point, but she was a creature of strict personal morals. "I cannot undress in front of a man."

The ghost voice sighed. "You have no idea how much it pains me to string these words together my dear, but would you, truly, consider me a man? Look at me."

Lisette spun around, half expecting to see someone, or something. There was only the darkness.

"There is nothing there," she said stiffly.

"Precisely. I am not a man. I am not, well, anything really, except my own thoughts. It's difficult to explain and even more difficult to experience. I don't recommend it."

"I expect not," Lisette said, turning her body so she sat with her back to the fire now. She was warmer, but he was right. The clothes had to go. "Turn around."

A warm chuckled sounded only a few feet away. "And if I don't?"

"See! You *are* a scoundrel!" Lisette exclaimed. "You do wish to see me undressed."

"Of course I do, you blithering fool. I haven't seen the female form in over eighty years. And yours, if my once flawless instincts on such matters are correct, is delectable."

"I won't do it," she tried to say firmly but her chattering teeth gave her away. She took a long, frustrated breath. She hated being wrong. "Oh alright. But don't- don't say anything. I wish you were a gentleman so you wouldn't look, but as long as it's like it never happened- and considering you don't exist- I'll just try and do behind the cabinet door and, and you just, just try not to look."

She rose and stumbled to the cabinet the ghost, which she had to admit was probably the best term for what, or whom, she was speaking to, had indicated. It was indeed beautiful. The dark mahogany doors were inlaid and carved into what appeared to be hunting scenes. They opened easily enough, and Lisette pulled out the blankets inside.

"And stay over there!" she called back in the direction of the fire, and, she hoped, the ghost.

She shook out a couple blankets and hung them over the cabinet doors, ready to encompass her the moment she was free of her wet, clinging clothes.

She peeled off her cloak and it fell to the floor with a heavy, wet thud. The rest took longer than usual to remove as it was all so damp and her hands were still a little numb, but she did it, shivering all the while.

Finally, she was wearing only her chemise. It was the most difficult to remove as the fabric was fine and worn and clung to her skin like a spider's web. She was little better than naked even with it on.

"Who says I'm not a gentleman?" the voice said, right behind her.

For only the second time that night, she screamed. "Oh you- you- you filthy minded rogue! You son of a-"

"Tsk tsk," the voice chided, sounding more and more like an old, amused friend. "Language, my dear. You called yourself a lady, but I have to doubt you if you speak like that."

"You have no room to talk," she said, pulling the blankets down and wrapping them around her naked body. The dust made her cough, but at least they were dry. "No gentleman would behave as you have done this evening."

An undeniable snicker came from the darkness. "For a lady you seem to have not met many gentlemen."

He had her there, but she would not let him know it. "To the contrary, I merely circulate in a, er, more refined set. Where I come from men do not gawk at naked women."

He laughed again, full and hearty and much warmer than before. The skill was returning quickly and Lisette thought he must have laughed often long ago.

"I do not believe that for a second," the voice finally said between lingering chortles, "and I will believe nearly anything at this point. I am a *ghost* for chrissakes."

"Laugh all you want, you still behaved terribly." Lisette said, settling down in the cavern of the inglenook before the blazing grate. She arranged the blankets around her, bundling one up into a pillow and nestling down against it. Now that she was finally warm, she felt utterly exhausted. Her eyes fluttered closed.

"I didn't look, you know."

Her eyes flew open. "You didn't?"

"No. Kept my gaze firmly averted. Unfortunately."

"How do I know that's true?"

She could practically hear his easy shrug. "You don't."

Lisette was going to say something to that, something clever and witty and-

But she said nothing, because she had made the mistake of closing her eyes again.

In moments she was so deeply asleep she never noticed the little breath of wind that stoked the fire. Not the first time, nor the second, nor any of the dozen times the same unseen force kept the flames burning merrily and warm before her.

And she certainly did not wake when that same otherworldly force rolled a couple of logs right past her sleeping form and placed them in the grate, clumsy but effective, nor when it pulled her blankets back around her after they fell a bit just before dawn.

Neither did she awake when, just as the morning's first light streamed in through the ancient grime-stained windows, a naughty gust of wind peeled back her blankets just enough to make out her now very dry, very warm, figure.

To the wind's credit, the blankets were immediately promptly put back.

The Manor

Lisette had never slept so deeply in her life. She stirred slightly, consciousness barely peaking into her mind. She felt warm, and very comfortable, wrapped in what felt like endless blankets, far softer than any back home. The floor was hard, but layers of wool softened the impact, and somehow she did not mind anyway.

She was so very tired. And so… something. Something had happened last night. Cold? Definitely. Afraid? Yes, at one point, she had been quite afraid, and then it all got very strange.

Lisette burrowed deeper into her nest, dimly aware of the sound of birds singing outside. Something felt different. It was a strange feeling, one she had not felt for a very, very long time.

It was a good feeling. Foreign, but nice. Like tasting a sweet she had loved as a child but had not tasted in many years.

Then it came to her, the name for the feeling and it seemed both obvious and sad she had not recognized it sooner.

She felt safe. She had not felt this safe since her parents had died, and she could barely remember what it felt like even then.

How she felt now was like that.

But warmer.

She gave a little sigh and rolled over onto her back. Slowly, she opened her eyes.

And shrieked.

A hideous, snarling face was just above her, bearing down. She leapt up, but was so tangled in the blankets she flailed for several moments before properly righting herself.

Looking back at the horrible creature, she saw now it was only the poorly rendered and very medieval face of a wolf carved into the inglenook fireplace where she had been sleeping.

Then it all came back to her.

The carriage ride. The highwaymen. The forest. The house. The wind and the voice and the lightning and then the ghost. Or, at least, a ghostly voice, but what was the difference?

Breathing hard, Lisette spun in a slow circle around the room. It looked like a perfectly acceptable drawing room, albeit a very grand and very old one. Dust and cobwebs covered everything, but somehow the massive windows were unbroken and no birds or forest creatures had made their way to nest inside. The place was simply old, abandoned... and beautiful.

The wood paneling that covered the walls extended up to the ceiling and across the high, vaulted space. Brass sconces shaped like tree branches and vines held up wizened candelabras. A chandelier made of antlers bigger than any she had ever seen crowned the center of the room.

The woodland theme was everywhere. Even the rugs on the knotted wood floor and the beyond aged furniture were all shades of green and brown. Tapestries the size of her uncle's entire sitting room hung on each side of the grand inglenook fireplace. One depicted the beginning of a hunt, and the other, its end. Both were far older and more impressive than any she had seen, and if she had to guess she would say they were some five hundred years old.

It took conscious effort to pull her mouth closed.

This was the grandest room she had ever seen.

Where was she?

As if on cue, her stomach growled.

Curiosity was one thing, hunger was another. She could not explore the house, let alone determine what to do next with her now utter shambles of a future, on an empty stomach. Her last meal had been at a coaching inn the morning before. It felt like a lifetime ago.

She took a step towards the door and froze.

As if living one of those dreams where one is asked to stand before the entire Sunday congregation only to realize one is not wearing anything, Lisette looked down and saw, to her horror, that while there was no congregation present, neither were her clothes.

"Damn!" she squealed, not caring if ladies did not use such language. This was as good a time as any for an emphatic expletive. Besides, she was completely alone.

In the light of day voices and spirits and ghosts were obvious for what they really were: nonexistent. It was evident with the morning's clarity that she had been so exhausted and terrified last night that she had hallucinated a whole host of phenomena. In fact, she may have dreamt most of it. She probably fell asleep by the fire, her mind off to the proverbial races. She would never know for certain, but that was alright, because she had survived the night. Not only that, the future was bright before her and, if she was clever enough to keep it this way, entirely her own.

She was intelligent enough and not completely untalented. Though she had had no official schooling she had taught herself to read and write better than anyone else she knew. She had no doubts that with only a few harmlessly fabricated recommendations, she could find a very agreeable position as a governess.

She would never marry the Marquess of Ulster or see her loathsome, spineless uncle, ever again.

But first, breakfast.

Well, firstly first, put on some clothes, and then…. Breakfast.

The clothing was by far the easy part. Lisette's things were hanging to dry along one wall of the inglenook where a series of iron hooks protruded from the stone.

Pulling down her blessedly dry things, Lisette marveled that she had been so exhausted that she remembered neither hanging them up nor stoking the fire in the night. But then, she had also been so utterly depleted that she had hallucinated a whole array of the most absurd events. Was it so difficult to believe that she had dried her clothes and kept the fire going?

Ever practical above all, Lisette decided it was not. It was all, as ever, perfectly reasonable. There was always a sensible explanation when one took the time to think of it.

Properly attired, she found her hairpin lying on a small table nearby and did her best to tame her unruly mop of curls. It was not an easy job. Then she neatly folded her blankets and stacked them to one side. The movements reminded her that she had fallen in her flight, but her knees and ankles were holding. Sore, yes. Injured… thankfully not.

These preliminaries completed, Lisette took a deep breath. She had to assess her surroundings, and the time of day, before she could decide on a plan. If it were later than she suspected another night might be in order. At least she had an understanding of the place so a second night would be far easier than the first.

Her stomach growled again. It was time to find some breakfast.

She turned the key in the lock and pulled open the heavy door, stepping boldly into the hall beyond.

It looked like a cyclone had torn the place apart. The front door was closed shut, but evidence of it having been open for some time was everywhere. Bits of leaves and dirt and an entire tree branch were strewn about on the floor, mixed in with what looked like chunks of stained glass and carved furniture.

She had not dreamt that bit, then.

"It was quite a storm," she mumbled, carefully making her way through the rubble. "Anything could have blown in through that door. It's perfectly reasonable."

Not knowing where the kitchens would be in a house such as this, she began opening every door that would budge.

Some were easier to open than others, and a few did not open at all, but none revealed a promising path to the kitchen. She did locate a sitting room, a hall even grander than the one she had slept in, which seemed to be some sort of gathering place or perhaps a ballroom, and a dining room. She also found a library but the door was one of the stuck ones and only opened enough for her to peer inside and see shelves of very dusty old books all the way to the ceiling.

She made a note of that for later, and eyeing the decrepit old staircase warily, decided the long narrow hallway tucked along one side of it was more promising.

Several nondescript rooms, some for storage, some for purposes she could not ascertain, met her along the way. This house was easily the largest she had ever set foot in, and despite its neglect, the nicest. She could easily have made due living in any of these rooms as her entire home. It was hard to fathom any one family requiring so much space.

The thought conjured an immediate fantasy. She could simply stay here. She would clean the place up, but only on the inside. The outside could remain untouched to keep up the facade that it was dreadful and haunted. That way no one would ever bother her here. Surely it would take years to get through that library even once, and if she sold only a few items of furniture she could live modestly in this grand old pile until the end of her days reading and, as there was obviously space for a garden, growing her roses.

The image, though impossible, cheered her, and Lisette felt particularly sunny as she reached the door at the end of the hallway.

Except, it was not a door. It was pieces of a door.

Someone, or something, had hacked brutally away at it. There was a massive hole ripped through the center of it, as if someone or something had been very desperate and very violent in its attempt to get through.

A chill went through Lisette, and she wondered if perhaps last night had not been her imagination after all.

Well, the voice and the ghost were, certainly, but the fear and the strangeness…. Perhaps not. Maybe there was some deep sense of the house that had given rise to her wilder imaginings. There was something dark in this place.

She would find food, take the blankets and whatever else was of use to her, and be gone. The storm had passed, so if she needed to shelter in the woods for a night, she could at least do that.

Gingerly, Lisette opened the mangled door. Beyond, finally, was the kitchen.

As Lisette entered the room, two things became immediately obvious: one, this place had not produced a meal since at least her grandfather's time, and two, she was not alone.

"Who did this?" she asked aloud, stepping up to a long, low wooden table in the center of the room.

There was no answer.

Lisette looked down at the basket before her. Inside was a loaf of fresh bread, an apple, and a wrapped package of what smelled intoxicatingly like smoked ham. Tucked beside these were two pasties, one that looked suspiciously like apple currant and the other, some sort of mincemeat.

She tapped the table with one finger as she considered her options. Someone had been here and left this food, which was obviously fresh, on the table. That very same someone might still be here.

That meant-

"Damn and blast," she scowled, taking the basket and nearly running back into the drawing room, locking the door behind her.

She was not going to look a gift horse in the mouth, even if that horse was not, in the end, meant to be a gift. Wait, did she have that right?

It didn't matter, because she had already taken a bite of the apple pasty and was rushing in a very unladylike manner to open the package of what was, blessedly, a very beautiful piece of smoked ham. It was all so delicious she nearly wept.

The entire spread was gone in ten minutes. All of it. It occurred to Lisette as she licked the last of the salty goodness from her fingertips that perhaps she should have kept some for later, because it was likely to be a long time before such a feast came her way again.

However, it was too late now. Too deliciously late.

She sat back for a moment to settle her stomach and gather her thoughts, grateful for the continued warmth of the fire.

It still crackled merrily and she marveled at how long-lasting the wood here was. Maybe she could simply start selling it, surely she could make a fortune off such premium-

She felt a prickling up her spine and her mind immediately focused on one single thought: she was not alone.

Had the person whose breakfast she stole come looking for it? For her?

Carefully, she rose.

Perhaps she was better off considering her options on the road. She would have plenty of time to decide things as she made her way through the forest, and if she left now, she would have most of the day ahead of her.

Quietly as she could, Lisette gathered the empty basket, the piece of flint, and the blankets. Glancing around the room, she guiltily took a silver candlestick, too. She had never stolen anything in her life, but then, she had never been this desperate. Surely, whoever owned this place had died so long ago it would not matter if a single piece of silver disappeared? This entire house had for all intents and purposes disappeared already.

With footsteps hushed by the dust on the floor, Lisette made for a window on the far end of the room. It was one of the few that had a latch and was just wide enough she could squeeze through it.

She heard nothing as she made her seemingly endless journey across the room, but she knew whoever she had sensed before was still nearby.

Worse, she felt whoever it was, was watching her.

It was odd that she had been so brave last night, but then, last night she had particularly desperate.

In the light of day she was certain of several things she had not been certain of last night. Namely, she was no longer in danger of freezing to death, and more pressingly, that ghosts were not real. That meant she could and should get away and, far worse, that whoever was watching her was real. *That,* she decided, was far more frightening than any apparition.

The window, much like everything else in the house, had not been touched in decades, perhaps centuries. It did not budge. She curled her fingers under the side that would open and pushed the panel with all her might.

Nothing.

The sense of being watched grew stronger. This did seem the type of place to have peep holes and secret passages, after all, and surely all those florid gothic novels got the idea somewhere? She could only see one door, but that did not mean it was the only one.

The thought sent a chill through her.

"Damn you, just open!" she growled at the window sill, giving it one more almighty heave. It creaked and pushed begrudgingly out.

She wanted to hoot for joy, but a cool voice stopped her.

"That's the third time you've used that word, by my count," the voice said, right behind her. "Are you sure you're a lady?"

Lisette, for the umpteenth time since her arrival, spun around. This time, however, was different. This time there was something behind her.

Or, more precisely, someone. A tall, strongly-built, and imposing someone.

Standing mere feet away from her, watching her with placid, assessing eyes the color of icy water, was a man. Or, at least, most of one.

From the waist up, he was broad-shouldered and finely built, like a man who spent as much time outside as in. His skin was the palest of pale and slightly translucent, but she thought it must once have been almost olive, another testament to time spent outdoors. High, chiseled cheekbones enhanced the unearthly aura of the man, as did the nearly perfect lines of his strong, slightly bent nose and perfectly full, firm lips. A mane of tousled dark hair fell to his shoulders, as unencumbered as the rest of him.

And unencumbered the rest of him was.

Perhaps it was for the best he was visible only from the waist up, as he appeared to be wearing nothing but a very flimsy nightshirt.

Lisette had always in the privacy of her mind mocked women who fainted. She assumed it was an act, and a boring and insipid one at that. Once, when a boy in the village had mocked her and asked her if she was going to faint after he put a toad in her bonnet, she had solemnly informed him that she would never, ever faint, and promptly connected her little fist to his rather bulbous nose.

She had been six.

Now, Lisette was twenty-one, a woman fully grown. She had learned great deal in the intervening years and grown to even greater heights of self-confidence and self-sufficiency. She had evolved far beyond even the no-nonsense harridan she had been in her youth. She was braver than ever.

That was why it took a full moment of stunned silence, as Lisette looked at the very handsome ghost floating in front of her, before she fainted.

The Host

Lord Peregrine Charles Aston, one-time Duke of Stafford, Marquess of Gloucester, and Baron Lyme, or, as he preferred, Perry, was amused.

It had been a very, *very* long time since anything had amused him.

"Well, my girl," he said to the inert body of the young woman on the floor below him, a tangle of shabby clothes and hair the color of the finest copper. "You do surprise me."

He floated slowly around her, wishing for perhaps the first time since his death that he could touch someone, if only to carry her to a more comfortable spot. That was, after all, the only reason *to* touch her. "Here I was, thinking you were so very brave, uncommonly brave, last night, and now one little fright and plop! There you go."

He waved a hand he knew no one could see in a dramatic flourish and smiled ruefully down at the lady who had utterly captivated him for the last twelve hours.

"If only I could hold you in my arms," he murmured to himself.

The lady's head shifted. "Whyever would you want to do that?" she asked, not as dazed as he would have wished.

Peregrine cleared his throat in the manner that had always reminded whoever was in earshot that he was a duke. "To pick you up from that pathetically ignoble position."

She stood immediately, all pride and lithe limbs. Not that her limbs mattered. Or, her pride. She would be gone soon, after all. "I'm not sure I be on my feet yet. I- I've never done that before."

"Stood up?"

She shot him a glare. "Fainted."

"Ah. That. It's a terribly common reaction, I'm afraid."

She was cross-legged on the old carpet now, her skirts tangled around her. She looked adorable, he thought. But then, he had always liked women, and he had not seen one in so long, this was like putting stale bread in front of a starving man. *Of course* he found her irresistible. He was a starving man! A starving man who could no longer eat.

"So," she began but he was immediately distracted. She wrinkled her nose when she was thinking hard, he noticed. He got the sense she had no idea she was doing it, or how adorable it was. "People usually faint when they see you?"

"Naturally, it's a jarring experience. One moment you think you understand the world and the next there's a ghostly voice-" Peregrine froze. "What did you say?"

The girl, who was really more of a woman, a young, perfectly-aged, beautifully formed, woman, rolled her eyes. "I see you're dead, do not tell me you also deaf? I asked if people usually faint when they see you or if it's just me"

Peregrine blinked once, then twice for good measure. "Er, no. I mean, they don't, you obviously did."

"Hmm. I find that difficult to believe. I'm quite fearless, more or less, so if *I* fainted, I can only imagine other people would-"

Peregrine could barely hear her. His world, which had long ago toppled off its axis, was shifting all over again. He voiced the only thing his mind could focus on. "You can see me?"

She looked at him as if he were an idiot. "Of course I can see you. Why do you think I fainted?"

"I- " Peregrine could honestly say it had been a century since he was last been at a loss for words. "I suppose I thought the sound of my voice startled you, as I had not spoken since last night and I was directly behind you. It's happened before. The startling, I mean."

She was looking at him like *he* was the madman. "That's ridiculous. I didn't faint last night, did I? I suspect it was too dark to see you then, but I can't imagine anyone seeing you for the first time and *not* having a significant reaction. Voices happen every day, but this?" She gestured at him. "It's disturbing."

"No offense," she added.

"None taken," Peregrine said, feeling a little dazed. He floated to a broad armchair and collapsed into it. Or, he would have, if he had any corporeal weight whatsoever. As it was, he just sort of leaned back, hovering a couple inches above the cushioned seat.

"Did I say something wrong?" she asked, concern making her bright green eyes sparkle. They shone bright as sunlight on new spring grass.

How had he not noticed sooner?

Now, he could not look away. She was *looking at him*. No one had looked at him, had seen him, since his death. Why should they? Ghosts were invisible.

Or, at least, he had thought they were.

"No, it's not you," he said. "It's me."

She raised a single, russet eyebrow.

Ignoring the perfect spray of delicate freckles across her nose, Peregrine cleared his throat. "I have been a ghost for over eighty years, and in that time, any number of people have come through this house. Or tried to, at least. My family did not abandon it for the first few years I was gone, so to speak, but I was angry then and did not know how to control myself. As my awarenesses returned but my manners did not, I drove them out."

"I'm sorry," she said. It was a reasonable thing to say, but it irked him. No one had ever been sorry for him. Why should they? He was the first son and heir of a duke. He was handsome, accomplished, charming, intelligent, as adept with a bow or sword as the lacings on any bodice, even the French ones. He was everything a man was supposed to be, but slightly better. Everyone thought so.

His only flaw for some time was that he was dead.

"Don't be," he bit out. "There's nothing to be done about it. I am here now, as you see, and sometimes locals or the curious or, more often, aspiring thieves, enter the house, and I set them to rights."

"You mean you terrify them into fleeing?"

"Precisely," he gave her a look of appreciation. She was lovely. It was not just the intelligence in her eyes or those damn freckles. It was all of her. She was divine feminine curves on a lithe frame, neither too tall nor too short. Just enough for a man to hold in all the best ways. Her bosom alone would have made him weep, if he were still capable of weeping. Not in front of her, obviously but....

He had never been so grateful for his invisibility as last night when he had watched her undress, or this morning, when she had awoken before remembering she was totally nude. She was a classical painting come to life. One of the really good ones, not like the dour old family portraits he owned. She was like the grand paintings of nymphs some of the naughtier artists in Paris came up with.

Gently curling waves of glistening auburn hair went down to her waist, in a fashion that as far as he could tell had long passed, but in his day had been the epitome of seduction. It made him a little hard just thinking about it. Well, as close as he could get given as he was made of ephemeral spirit, but he *felt* hard.

Which, on reflection, was awful. This line of thought was only an exercise in pain and embarrassment. More idiot he for slavering over a living, breathing woman when he would never touch one again.

Sometimes he hated being dead.

"Now my dear," he said, floating back up and adding extra disinterest to his tone in case she had sensed the direction of his ill-advised thoughts, "if you don't mind, given my failure to accomplish this in the usual way, I must deign to ask you, politely, to leave."

"Excuse me?"

"Now." He pointed to the door, making a mounted set of antlers crash to floor on the other side of the room, just for emphasis.

His unwanted guest gazed up at him, that thoughtful furrow in her brow.

It made him uneasy. It made him harder. *Damn and blast.*

Obviously, he had been haunting the attic for too long again and forgotten himself. No woman had ever unsettled him or made him uneasy. Oh, they had tried. One mistress in particular came to mind. She had tried to shatter a mirror over his head. She had not succeeded however, in unsettling him, or the bit with the mirror.

"Apologies but no," his unwanted visitor said bluntly. "I'm not leaving yet."

Peregrine thought he may have misheard her, but she did not move.

He floated closer, in part to intimidate, in part because, damn him, he wanted to. "You will leave here. Immediately. Take the blankets and whatever else you wish, I don't care. Just. Go."

He stopped mere inches from her. She had not budged. He looked down at her, willing his voice into its most ducal and commanding. "There is a hidden compartment in the smaller drawing room with a very fine sapphire ring in it and, fortunately for you, I am feeling generous today. Take it, and go. I will not say it again."

The lady's eyes darted to the door, then returned to his and narrowed. "Neither shall I. I am not leaving today."

"Yes, you are," he said, his voice strengthening.

"No I'm not!" she said in a tone to match.

Peregrine had never been a patient man in life, and he certainly was not one now. "GET OUT OF THIS HOUSE!" he shouted as only someone who's only ever known complete obedience can. "NOW!"

"I'M NOT LEAVING!" she shouted back.

The Ghost Duke Who Loved Me

Their faces, hers flushed and rosy, his translucent and slightly shimmering, were mere inches from one another.

This was the moment to kiss her, Peregrine thought unbidden. Even after all these years his skill with women was too well-honed to miss an opportunity like this. Passion was rolling off her in waves so hot he could nearly feel it, and he could not feel anything.

If only he were flesh and blood- he stopped. That way lay misery. What was done was done.

"Why not?" he asked quietly, his voice harsh and tellingly ragged.

Her lips parted in surprise. She was young, yes, but not unaware of the frisson between them. God he wanted to kiss-

"It is nearly dark," she said, taking a step back, a hitch in her own breath. It was her first retreat, he noted. "The rain has returned, and I am not going anywhere until tomorrow."

He floated back what would have been a step. "What do you mean? It's only midday."

They both looked to the tall windows where the towering forest was, indeed, darkened by the fading daylight and a drizzle of cold rain was falling. His brow furrowed. "What the devil- but you only fainted a moment ago."

"Apparently not," she shrugged, a pretty little gesture. Her shoulders were fine and delicate, belying what he was coming to suspect was a ferocious character. "I don't know why you are so surprised, you're not the one who spent several hours unconscious on the floor."

"It was only a moment," Peregrine murmured.

"Obviously death has affected your sense of time, if you don't mind my saying so," she said and walked off, back to the fireplace, which was cold. "As for me, I suppose I was so exhausted from last night that once I hit the ground, I stayed a while."

Peregrine was only half listening, however. How had he lost track of time? He never gave time much thought, as he had no particular reason to, but now that he thought on it he realized his awareness of time's passage had become imperceptibly twisted. What had felt to him like a few minutes had in fact been several hours. At this rate they would be well into the next century before he even noticed. She was right, death was affecting him in ways he had not realized, and would not have realized perhaps ever, had her very much alive and observant self blundered into his well-ordered afterlife.

"Is something wrong?" she asked. Her voice was a little lower than one would expect by looking at her, a little huskier. It was set off by the natural kindness in her eyes in a way he liked. She was not a boring person, which was good. He despised boring people. "Whatever you're thinking about, it won't work. I'm not leaving until morning."

"No. I mean yes, that is-" Peregrine stammered, again uncharacteristically struggling for words like an untried schoolboy, "nothing is wrong. You're welcome to stay. I was only thinking."

She gave him an appraising look from the fire, which she was starting up again. "It makes you look dangerous."

"When I think?"

"Yes," she answered slowly. Then, "Am I losing my mind?"

If there was one question Peregrine had asked himself more than any other in the last eighty years it was that one. Of course when you awake one morning to find yourself nothing but a sort of thicker type of air, floating around your own house, screaming and shouting to everyone you know and no one can hear you, one is apt to question ones sanity. As the years passed he stopped questioning anything.

"No," he replied simply, floating over to her. He was careful not to get too close. He had figured out over the decades that if he was too near a living person he made them feel cold, and he did not wish that for her. In fact, he gave a little blow and the sparks she was working with billowed into merrily crackling flames.

"How do you do that?" she asked, eyes wide in wonder.

"I have no idea."

There was that brow furrow again. Damn him, he liked it.

Only because she was the first female whose company he had shared in decades, but still, it was…. charming.

"You don't know how you do things? I mean, unusual, ghostly things? Because that's what you are, isn't it?"

"I'm afraid so," Peregrine said, feeling the weight of it. God, he was so tired. It was was true what they said, about spirits being restless. He had not truly rested since the night before he died. "Sometimes I can move things about, but it drains me, and its not always precise. I can go as far as the edge of the estate, but the further I get from the house the weaker I become. I have figured out a few things like that, but I don't know the why or the how of it."

"May I ask, sir," she hesitated, and he decided he liked her when she was unsure just as much as he enjoyed her confidence, "how did it happen? You becoming a ghost, I mean?"

A flash of memory, sharp and painful and embarrassing, went

through him.

"I don't remember," he lied. "What is your name?"

If she knew he misled her, she did not let on. She merely nodded and said, "*I* am Lady Lisette Havens, of Derbyshire. My father was a baronet, but a very poor one, and my mother was a local gentleman's daughter. They both died when I was six. Fever took them. I don't think they're ghosts, though."

"I'm sorry to hear that- about their deaths, I mean. I would be happy to know they are not trapped between worlds like me."

"It's that bad?"

Peregrine had never talked to anyone about what it was like. Why would he? His sole ambition any time anyone came near the old house was to get them away as quickly as possible. The company of the living only made him feel all the more dead. Besides, he was fine without human companionship. He had taken up a rather pathetic habit of speaking to the owl in the westernmost eaves of the attic, but the conversation was terribly dull and generally one-sided.

"It's a very lonely existence," he said, unable and unwilling to answer the genuine curiosity he saw in her eyes. "I am Peregrine, by the way. Peregrine Charles Aston, Duke- well, *former* Duke- of Drayton."

Her eyes grew the widest he had yet seen them. "You're a Duke?"

"I *was* a duke. Yes."

Her jaw dropped and his fingers twitched with the urge to gently shut it for her.

God, he was pathetic- one passable sprig of muslin enters the house and he is melting over her. He needed to remember himself, his position- both the ducal and the deceased varieties.

"No more questions," he said sternly, rising and floating to the edge of the firelight. "You may stay tonight and no more. I shall wake you at dawn if you are not already leaving. Goodnight, Miss Havens."

"Goodnight, Your Grace."

"Peregrine," he said without thinking.

She looked surprised, and he wanted to kick himself but he had no legs. He was turning into a damned milksop.

"Goodnight then, Peregrine."

The words were softly spoken, but they sent a chill through him.

Which was ridiculous.

The fire gave a loud pop, and she turned to adjust a crackling log.

When she glanced back, he was gone.

The Guest

Two Days Later

"He looks terribly grumpy, who is he?"

Peregrine took in the glowering face of the portrait Lisette indicated. "My grandfather, actually."

Her brow wrinkled. "You look nothing like him. Are you sure?"

Peregrine chuckled for the umpteenth time that day. "Sadly yes. There is no doubting it, but I appreciate your disbelief. He was by all accounts an angry drunk, and he drank all the time."

"Unfortunate," was Lisette's only reply. She continued down the hallway.

They were upstairs admiring portraits in the hall. It was part of a thorough tour of the house Peregrine had begun the day before. He had assured Lisette that this was not a large house and that his other residences had been far larger. This was merely his favorite hunting lodge, one of three such properties he had possessed in his lifetime.

Peregrine's easy dismissiveness of the house's grandeur was not the only thing that had baffled Lisette in the last two days. If she were being honest with herself everything had been turned upside down from the moment she had first arrived at the house.

Lisette had never believed in ghosts or goblins or anything supernatural. She had not even been particularly devout when it came to the far more serious matter of her eternal soul. More than once she had feigned headache on a Sunday morning only to spend those preciously quiet hours in the garden or reading a distinctly non-Biblical book.

Of course sometimes her imagination carried her into a fanciful daydreams or imagining that she would one day be rescued by sudden message that she had secretly been a grand heiress all along. Lonely young women often imagined themselves rescued by surprise turns of fate, she supposed. Such flights of fancy were perfectly natural.

In all, Lisette had always had two feet firmly planted on good, sensible English soil. She knew she was not a secret heiress, just as she knew there were no gnomes in the garden and if there was a god above he probably did not care if she missed services so long as she was a good person. Any flights of fancy in which she indulged were perfectly harmless and sensible. She had certainly never been so lonely as to imagine any of it was *real*, and she absolutely would never fancy herself friends with a ghost.

Until now.

In the last few days she had worried more than once that she was losing her mind, but Peregrine was such charming company Lisette decided that if this was insanity, she would happily accept her fate. Talking to thin air in a massive and fascinating old house was far better than a dreary, aimless life with her uncle, or- the real alternative- the nightmare of being the Marchioness of Ulster.

It was funny how life could shift so suddenly and in such unexpected directions. Even that first evening she and Peregrine had properly met one another, he had been so gruff and eager for her to leave. She had fallen asleep fitfully, anxious about her next steps and whether she was mad. In the morning, however, he had been floating nearby. She'd sat up, afraid she had slept in and he was about to do something dreadful, but he didn't. He floated over to her and, guessing correctly that she wanted breakfast, told her where the fresh food came from.

Apparently a few of the local villagers brought offerings to the house to assuage the spirits, leaving a basket of fresh bread, fruit, meat, and any excess they could scrape together in an alcove at the old stone gate. Peregrine had explained that over the years he'd been in a foul enough mood to ensure anyone who lived within five miles of the house was utterly terrified of it. They seemed to think if they left food and gifts at the front gate the spirits would not venture further than the estate. They had no idea the particular spirit in question had no desire to go anywhere at all.

Yesterday Peregrine had gone to the gate, which was, he explained, as far afield as he could travel, and clumsily used whatever powers he possessed to float the food into the kitchen. Impressed, Lisette had asked him to demonstrate by floating whatever was out there just then into the house and straight over to the fireplace where she sat.

He had laughed and informed her that his powers were not reliable, unless you counted how utterly exhausted using them always left him. If he had attempted to bring the food in there was no guarantee it would not spill everywhere, but he had no doubt the attempt would render him unable to give her a proper tour of the house.

So Lissette was not evicted after all. Instead, she had gone to get the food herself- half a cake and a single apple- and returned to spend the entire day wandering the ground floor of the hunting lodge listening to Peregrine's endless tales of his and his family's escapades. It had been one of the best days of her life.

Which only marked how dull her life was, she reminded herself. Of course Peregrine was charming and made her feel alight, like she was the center of the world. He was, though formless spirit, a gentleman, which was a novel treat for Lissette, who only knew a few boys from the village, all of whom were just as dull as her life there had been. Peregrine, she was sure, made her feel so important only because she was the only person he had talked to in decades.

Anyway, he did not spend *every* moment with her. They would spend a few hours at a time to themselves. Usually he would just disappear, but sometimes he would give some reason for it, like a sound somewhere far off that needed his investigating. It was curious, the way he came and went, but she never asked about it. She was happy for any time he was hovering nearby, telling her about his ancestor who shot wildly into the woods after what he believed was a unicorn only to find out it was a neighbor's fencepost.

The time alone also gave her a chance to process everything- and there was a lot to process.

For instance, she had been mistaken at first that he was merely visible from the waist up. Today, she realized as they stood in the portrait hallway, she could almost make out his knees. The tops of legs clad in nondescript breeches, far looser than any gentleman of her acquaintance would wear, were just visible beneath the hem of his loose and half-open nightshirt. It was a curious look and made him appear slovenly, though she would never tell him that.

Nor would she ask why he was dressed that way. She was careful not to ask too many questions about his current state or what had led up to it. It seemed impolite to ask such things and she sensed Peregrine would rather not discuss them anyway. She could not blame him. Surely dying was not something one would wish to relive, so to speak.

Instead he had asked her about her life, about her always laughing father and her quiet, kind French mother. He asked her about her childhood and, when he learned of her love of roses, he asked her the names and nature of her favorite kinds. She explained her desire to have a garden of her own and a home by sea, though she had never seen it.

When she told him how she came to be in his house and the dreadful marriage that awaited her if she were found Peregrine told her to stay as long as she liked.

She was grateful for his offer and his questions, but she preferred when he spoke about himself. He was, being a ghost aside, a terribly fascinating person. He told her of his many travels. He had seen Italy and France, Portugal and Germany, even as far as Romania and several countries she had never heard of that rolled off the tongue like incantations. She supposed such explorations were just what any young duke ought to have done, though Peregrine assured her that in his day it was a rare thing. He never told her why he had traveled so far, if it was an unusual thing to do, and as with so many topics, she did not ask. He was a private man, or ghost, rather, and she was patient. After all, the stories he did tell her of growing up in Stafford House in Sussex with servants and dogs and visiting princes, it was enough to placate even her active mind.

"And this one, who is she? I have never seen eyes so black, like a raven's." They had moved further along the gallery now and were both looking up at a startling portrait of a woman with hair like midnight and a smile that spoke of secrets. Lisette found her unsettling.

"That's my mother," Peregrine said, a trace of warmth in his voice Lisette had not heard before.

"Really? She seems so young."

"She was. Her people were Romani. Travelers. She was only fifteen when she married my father, and I was born the following year."

Lisette looked at him aghast. "That's- that's too young. She was still a girl!"

"Yes, she was very young, but that was how it was done. I wasn't there and neither of my parents ever spoke of it. They barely spoke to each other let alone about one another."

Lisette let that sink in. She knew little of the aristocracy, and certainly not what they had been a century ago, but she knew enough to question him. "Your father was a duke, and he married a woman of no standing? No title or birth? That he did not even wish to speak to? How was that possible?"

A shadow passed over his features, making him look like the flickering light of a torch. "He had a special dispensation from the king," he said, and she could tell this was another topic he wished to leave alone. She decided this time she would not let him avoid her questions.

"The king knew her age and allowed it? Maybe you are far older than I guessed, because that sounds like the actions of a medieval king. She was not even English was she? Was he in love with her when they wed?"

Sidestepping the last question, Peregrine returned curtly, "An aristocrat's wife need not be English. Your mother was French."

He was irritated. Lisette knew she was treading dangerous ground, but her curiosity demanded she know more. He was hiding something important. She could sense it.

"Yes, my mother was from Paris," she said, "but my father was the lowest an aristocrat could be and still count himself a gentleman. It was hardly a scandal. No one cared what he did, especially the king. But if he had been a duke, so close to the throne, and she, a Romani woman, their marriage would never have been allowed."

"There were special circumstances," Peregrine snapped, his voice tighter and more ducal. He was used to being obeyed, not questioned. "Everyone involved thought that someone of her birth and.... understanding, would be ideal for my father."

Lisette was now more confused, and curious, than ever.

"But she was so young! What kind of understanding could she-"

"Enough!" he commanded, fully the duke. "We will not speak of it any more. It was a long time ago. Now if you will excuse me I sense a rat in the east wing doing some damage to one of the gutters."

Lisette opened her mouth to argue, but he was already gone, like a tendril of smoke in a gentle breeze. Lisette doubted very much that there were any rats tampering with any gutters.

She rolled her eyes, hoping he could sense that too, and continued her exploration down the hall.

That evening Peregrine did not join her by the fire. He had offered her use of any of the bedrooms upstairs but they were all so very lonely, she preferred the grandness and warmth of the inglenook fireplace in the drawing room. That is what he called it. As if it were a drawing room like any other. She thought the cavernous space was more a great hall from the ancient stories of knights and dragons. It was nothing like any drawing room she had ever known, but then, Peregrine had seen much more of the world and knew far more about such things. She doubted he knew anything about gardening, goats, or chickens, but then those things were hardly glamorous to an outsider.

Their lives, when lived, were so very different. Peregrine's had been grand and sophisticated and important. Hers was… contemplative. That was probably the most flattering term for it. It was curious though, the differences, given that in living years they were not far apart in age. He had obviously died young, sometime in his twenties, if Lisette had to guess. But then there were all the years he had not been alive….

She had still not determined exactly when he had died, but her best guess was about a century ago. That would explain the portraits of his parents and a few of his offhand comments about the house and himself.

His age was curious thought. Even with his ghostly and incorporeal appearance she could tell he was only a few years older than Lisette herself, yet he spoke like a much older man. Lisette assumed it was because his mind was so much older than what shimmering residue remained of his body. It made it difficult to understand him, his exterior, or what there was of it, was so at odds with the sardonic wisdom underneath. Was he truly eighty years old? An hundred? More?

Lisette could not help wondering what his life would have been like had he lived longer.

It was a shame to die so young. Tragic for anyone, but Peregrine was not just anyone. He was a duke, and moreover, he was a terribly charming, wickedly smart and distractedly handsome duke. It was not fair.

She wondered, and not for the first time, if he had been married. He never mentioned a wife or children, but that meant nothing. There was so much he was not telling her.

Maybe it was better that way, she thought, taking a bite of one of the hand pies that had been left at the gate yesterday. They were still delicious, especially after she warmed them by the fire. It was a pity she could not stay here much longer.

But maybe that was better this way, too. Peregrine had said she could stay as long as she liked, but she could not truly live in an abandoned estate with only a ghost for company, could she? It was better than marriage to Ulster, or even living with her uncle, but there was no future in it. And if she made the place truly habitable then surely others would come and claim it and cast her out, and even Peregrine would not be able to stop them.

Lisette took another bite and decided to think of happier things. She would stay here another day or two at most, and then she would be off to build a new future for herself.

After dinner she read for a while, curled in the nest of cushions and blankets she had cleaned and arranged against the seats of the inglenook. Tonight's literature was a book on the local fauna of the region, which seemed just the sort of book one should keep in a hunting lodge. It was written long ago in an old style that quickly put Lisette to sleep.

It was hours later in the very dead of night when Lisette awoke to a horrible crashing sound, like the house was collapsing around her.

She sat bolt upright, immediately awake.

The dim light of the sliver of moon outside was enough to show her that the house was not collapsing, or at least, not this part. The drawing room was still and undisturbed.

"Maybe just a dream," she mumbled, hoping it was true.

A second horrible crash, louder than the first, shook the house.

"Damn and blast," she muttered, the epithet the only thing she was happy to borrow from her uncle, in part because he would hate to ever hear her use it.

Rousing enough sparks from the still hot embers to light a nearby candle, Lisette took the dim illumination and walked into the hall.

A third crash shook the house, this one paired with an agonized cry. It sent a chill down Lisette's spine.

She knew she had been talking to a ghost for three days, but she had not been afraid since that first night. Not since she had learned that the ghost was anything but scary.

Perhaps she had been wrong.

She approached the broad stairs and went up. The noise had been high, somewhere near the top of the house.

As she reached the landing another thundering crash and the sound of shattering glass broke the night, a cry of utmost pain echoing into the enveloping stillness. The sounds were coming from the attic.

Lisette had not been to the attic. That was the only part of the house off limits. Peregrine had personally taken her everywhere else, told her about the history of the house, how it had been in his family for generations ever since an ancestor won it in an ill-advised card game. He was proud of every inch of it- she believed him when he said this was his favorite of the many houses he had once owned. She could tell he delighted in showing it to her.

But the attic was his and his alone. He had made her swear on the very first day not to step foot there.

Lisette considered herself an honorable woman, but some promises were meant to be broken.

She made for the attic.

She had seen the servants stairs and knew that from this level the attic was one more narrow, worn flight up.

While what sounded like a series of small explosions cascaded above, Lisette took a steadying breath and ascended the creaking, broken stairs.

Her first impression was dust. A lot of dust. Her candle fought to light further than a foot ahead of her in what seemed to be a blinding sandstorm of dust.

Another scream of pain rent the silence, accompanied with what sounded like a pianoforte being thrown across the room. Lisette shuddered. The very air vibrated with anger and pain. She knew instinctively she should not be here.

She took a careful step forward. The board beneath her foot groaned and suddenly the dust moved and twisted and gathered before her, darkening into a black writhing mass.

Her own scream caught in her throat at the horror of it and the agonized howl that grew and grew from it, surrounding her, wind stronger and more terrifying than anything conjured that first night wrapped around her, tearing at her hair and clothes.

She turned to leave but caught her toe painfully on a loose board. Lisette tumbled to the floor, her candle snuffed out by the fall and the maelstrom of anger spiraling around her.

She began to cough now, the dust catching in her lungs, filling her nostrils. Everything was darkness and she could barely breathe. She tried to will herself to get up and flee but not even the dim light of the moon penetrated this forgotten space, and the darkness of the spirit that dwelled here was all around her, screaming.

"GETTT OUTTTTTTT," she heard, the words torn away as soon as they reached her ears, as if they were coming from far away in the heart of a storm. "LEAVVEEEEEE MEEEEEE..."

The effect was terrifying, or should have been, but the sound of the voice brought Lisette back to herself, and the truth:

There was only one ghost here.

Peregrine heard a voice, as if from a long way off. A woman calling out to him, as if from the heart of a storm.

"Peregrine!"

He wanted to answer. He wanted to go to her, to find the owner of the voice. She was safe, he knew that. He wanted her, he wanted that safety, that voice...

"Peregrine! Come back!" Her voice was firm and brave, braver than he was by far, and resolutely more constant. A rock in the sea where he cast adrift.

How was it that even in the darkness that consumed him he enjoyed a well-wrought analogy? Too much bloody poetry in his youth. He chuckled, or rather, felt the sensation of a chuckle pass through him.

"It's not funny. I am not going anywhere!" the voice said, closer now and a little angry.

He did not want to anger her.

Her?

A face, heart-shaped and fair with a perfect spray of freckles across the nose, appeared in his mind. *Her.*

Eyes glimmering like the brightest emeralds reached him through the fog. *Her.*

The old feeling that he was descending from on high and coming together at the same time overtook him. He wished he had the words for it, what it was like living this half life, this in-between existence. The only words he had were clumsy, but he supposed "coming back together" was an acceptable way of thinking about it. He could not very well say coming back to earth when he had not touched the stuff in nearly a century.

Then, as suddenly as always, he was back. And *she* was there. Lisette was standing before him, breathing heavily in nothing more than her shift, hair more unruly than ever before, as if she had been caught in a cyclone.

"You called?" he asked in his driest tone. She did not need to know the effect she had on him, that he was concerned for her and what she had witnessed. She also did not need to know that her wildly disheveled and obviously concerned presence was giving him sensations he had not felt in decades, sensations he could do nothing about. She did not need to know any of that.

"I did," she said.

Perry looked her up and down. "You look terrible."

Lisette's eyebrows rose and he was certain he had crossed a line. Then, glorious, unexpected being she was, she laughed.

"*I* look terrible? I look terrible!" she repeated, cackling like a madwoman and looking like pure sin. Good god, if he had a body…

"Why are you disturbing me in my attic?" he asked, better to change the subject.

It didn't help. She stopped laughing and rounded on him. "Why did you wake me up with your- your caterwauling like an angry babe? I thought the house was coming down around me."

"What are you talking about? I did no such thing. You are the one who came up here and started shouting at me."

"You were howling!"

"Howling? My dear girl, I was *sleeping*, or, well, I think it's as close as I get- it's- difficult to explain."

She looked at him in shock. "You really don't know?"

"Don't know what? All I know is I was…. occupied… elsewhere… and then here you are shouting at me. Why don't you dust yourself off and go back to bed?"

Lisette stared. She couldn't help it. He wasn't joking. He really had no idea what had happened. It was hard to believe, but then, how would he know? Who would tell him? Owls and mice and rats certainly could politely inform him, let alone not ask the questions that needed asking.

"Where were you?"

He blinked. It was odd, between her eyes adjusting to the darkness and the faint luminescence he emitted as he floated before her, she could nearly see all of him, clearer than ever. She could almost make out his feet, floating a few inches off the floor. He was even taller than she had guessed. Well, he had been.

"It's none of your business where I was," he replied like a surly schoolboy. Something was up. Again.

"When you were 'occupied', what were you occupied *with*? Just now," Lisette said, not backing down.

He shrugged, avoiding her gaze. "Sometimes I go…. elsewhere."

Lisette sighed in frustration. "Yes, but *where*? Do you know what's happening here when you…. do that?"

Lisette did not know a ghost could grow paler, but Peregrine did. "No."

"The entire house was filled with screaming. It was shaking from the attic to the foundation. Things were being thrown everywhere. How do you think this happened?" She gestured to what was, in fact, a shattered pianoforte crumpled against one wall.

"Ah. That," Peregrine said, "is unfortunate."

Lisette did not know what to make of it. He seemed both genuinely confused, even dazed, and strangely resigned.

"You are the only spirit in the house, aren't you?"

He nodded. "I am. And I- well, perhaps I owe you some explanations. Please, sit down." He waved a vague hand in the darkness.

"I agree, but can we go downstairs first? I'm cold."

He looked surprised again, having obviously forgotten about things like being cold. "I imagine so," he said, his eyes raked down her body and Lisette realized she had run upstairs without anything more than her thin night rail. No wonder she was shivering.

The heat in his clear gaze had nothing to do with it, she told herself. After all, he was a ghost, surely if he could not feel the cold he had no use for earthly desires, either.

All the same, she wrapped her arms around her bosom to hide the hardening evidence of what she reminded herself was the cold. They went downstairs.

Once back to the inglenook, Lisette started the fire back up and wrapped herself in her collection of blankets. Peregrine, for his part, hovered closer than usual, cross-legged and about three inches off the ground. Even in the flickering firelight he was still not as translucent as usual. He was so defined now she could almost pretend he was really there.

Almost.

"You do know what happened upstairs, don't you?" she asked quietly.

"I do."

The Curse

"Does it happen often?"

He sighed, weighing his answer. Weighing if he would answer. When he finally spoke it was with such gravity Lisette swore he sank an inch closer to the floor.

"I call it the Darkness," he said, staring into the fire. "When I died I did not realize it, at first. It was not like a children's story where you are floating over yourself watching everyone below. Nothing like that. Maybe it is different for others, if there are others."

"What *was* it like?" she said so quietly the words could barely be heard, but he heard them.

"It happened in the middle of the night, quite suddenly. I was in bed. There was a sudden staggering pain, worse than anything I had ever known."

Lisette was barely breathing herself now, listening to his words. His gaze had not left the fire and he spoke like a man entranced.

"What then?" she asked, dreading the answer.

"Then nothing. Just black, endless, unknowable, black."

Lisette worried her lower lip, trying to imagine what he was describing. She could not. "Sounds horrible."

"It was pleasant enough, actually." His mouth curled rueful smile before his face returned to its stony contemplation. "It felt like nothing and everything all at once. I had no sense of myself, of time, of anything, but the void. Eventually I began to know again, to think in stops and starts. That was far worse. It was like a dream when you begin to suspect you're dreaming but cannot seem to alter or escape it. Things carried on like that for a long while."

"Were you afraid?"

He met her eyes then. His were cold and fierce and she saw the powerful man he once had been, had been raised to be, in that knowing gaze. She shuddered.

"No," he said. "Not yet."

She nodded and he looked back to the fire.

"I eventually determined that I was in that void for nearly three months before I returned, or came to, or however we should consider it. My funeral was long over. Shame I missed it, honestly. They just did it here in the chapel on the edge of the grounds and buried me in the ancient plot beside it, underneath an oak nearly as old as the house."

"It sounds lovely," Lisette said, unsure what exactly one ought to say.

"It is. I was not strong enough in this state to visit my grave for many years, but I did visit it once, just to know I was not mad. I half expected not to find it, but of course, it was there, epitaph and all."

"What did it say?"

"Death be not proud."

"Ah. That's… erm…."

Perry grimaced. "There's no need to be kind about it. It's terrible joke my brothers no doubt were very proud of. It is a line from John Donne, one of our favorite poets."

"You and your brothers enjoyed poetry?"

"Don't get any romantic notions now. We did not enjoy poetry, we enjoyed *Donne*. He wrote a lot of naughtiness, you see."

"Oh, I know. I adore Donne, amongst others. I am not so selective as you, my dear Lord Condescension. *'I wonder, by my troth, what thou and I did, till we loved?'*"

Perry chuckled. "That's the one. My brothers obviously thought they selected the appropriate passage given the circumstances of my demise."

"Your brothers sound very wicked."

"None of us got along particularly well, unless we were tormenting one of our own. I've had years now to think on it, and that is perhaps my one regret, that I did not give them the regard and love that brothers ought to share."

The words spilled out unbidden, but as soon as he uttered them, Perry knew they were true.

"That is beautiful, and very sad," said Lisette. "Do you know what happened to them?"

"No," Perry said shortly. "I never saw or heard tell of any of my family ever again."

The Ghost Duke Who Loved Me

There was a long silence then, thoughtful but not uncomfortable. She had only known him a few days but there was something in him, a mix of his sincerity, his humor, and some depths of hard won wisdom, that made her feel as if she had known him all her life.

"Do you know how it happened?" she finally asked.

"I told you," he replied testily. "It was late at night, there was a sharp pain, and then-"

"No, I mean, how did you become a *ghost*," she said seriously. "I'm sure if it happened to everybody we would know, wouldn't we? Richard the Lionheart and Julius Caesar would still be giving speeches and wreaking havoc, surely."

He knew what she was really asking. He heaved another sigh that brought him so low and so near he was almost touching the floor, and, more distractedly, almost touching her knee where it bent towards him. Though she was covered in blankets and he had no solid form, she wondered what it would be like to touch him.

She wished suddenly, and with great force, that she could. Her hand twitched, seeking to reach out to him and-

He spoke.

"I know you have spent the last few days in the company of an undead spirit trapped in limbo, but I don't suppose you believe in curses?"

"Curses?" she said, genuinely surprised. Her hand stilled. "You were *cursed*? Who cursed you? A witch? Are there witches too? And, and don't tell me there are dragons and fairies and-"

Peregrine was laughing now, the warmth of his rich, deep voice washing over her. "No, no, my dear, don't get ahead of yourself. I think we would all know if dragons were real, they'd be rather hard to miss I imagine, and as for fairies, so far as I know they are pure fiction. Stuff for children and nothing more."

Lisette noticed what he did not say. "And witches?"

"Those, I'm afraid, are quite real."

Lisette swore the fire flickered then, as if the very air around them shuddered at the knowledge. "You're having me on, Your Grace. You've persuaded me into believing you're real, but if you think I will believe in old crones in the woods bartering rat tails and toad eyes in exchange for love potions, you have me quite wrong."

"Who is talking about old crones and nasty animal bits?"

"You are," Lisette said. "You just told me witches are real."

He laughed again and Lisette wished she could hear that sound every day for the rest of her life.

Which was a stupid, and wholly unnecessary thought.

"They are real, but they are not old crones or even terrifying sorceresses, as far as I know. In fact, I've always heard they're quite lovely. That makes them far more dangerous, as you can imagine."

Lisette's brow furrowed. "You've heard? You mean, you've never met one but you know they exist? How did they curse you if-"

"Slow down, my love!" he said, and the last word rocketed through her like lightning. It meant nothing, it was just a manner of speech, but the sound of it made her knees weak. He obviously didn't notice, as he continued on, "Let me explain. *I* am not the recipient of the curse, I am merely… cursed by a curse. Does that make sense?"

"Not at all. You are terrible at explanations, Your Grace."

"Hardly, and stop calling me that. It's Peregrin for most, and Perry for you."

"Very well, then, Perry, you are very poor at explaining things."

"Only when beautiful women keep interrupting me."

Those words rocketed through them both and Lisette had the distinct impression he had not meant to say them aloud. He looked back to the fire immediately, and she did the same. Clearing his throat, he continued, "What I mean to say is, my ancestor was cursed, long ago. The curse has carried down the male line of my family ever since, and we only have sons. It killed my father, it killed me, and I assume it also destroyed my brothers. I do not know, as none of them ever came here again after I died and there was no way to learn of their doings."

Lisette's mind whirled with questions, but only one made it past her lips. "Who was the witch?"

"Ah, you might not believe this bit…" he glanced at her, mischief glinting in the corners of his increasingly blue eyes. Lisette knew it was only her growing fondness for him, but he felt more real every moment they sat together. It was nice. Dangerous in ways she did not want to think about just yet, but nice.

"In for a penny, in for a pound," she grinned. "So who was she?"

"Anne Boleyn."

Lisette was grateful both that she was sitting and that she was not holding a tray of heirloom china, because this was just sort of the revelation that would have caused her to topple over and destroy it all. "Not *the* Anne Boleyn?"

"The very same."

"The one who was alive over three hundred years ago? Wife of

Henry VIII? The one he nearly destroyed the kingdom over?"

"That's her."

Lisette let that sink in a moment. "Anne Boleyn, a witch! One does hear the rumors, don't they?"

"Most are hogwash. She had some powers, obviously, but hardly what the histories claim and she did *not* have six fingers. Nothing so flagrant. From what I've been told there are not many who can actually practice witchcraft and those that do generally hide it for obvious reasons."

"And yet she really did curse your ancestor. Why?"

"Well, that is a part of her legend that does seem to be accurate. She was a profligate lover and wildly jealous, which is a terrible combination. She must have been magnificent in bed to make up for it, those sorts of people generally are. Good lovers, I mean."

"I wouldn't know," Lisette said as heat wholly unrelated to the fire warmed her cheeks.

Catching himself, Perry looked at her. "No, I suppose not. Not yet anyway."

Lisette felt her stomach drop and a rush of anticipation rippled through her. "But you can't touch me, can you?"

Perry blinked. "That's not what I-" he began and Lisette realized he had not been referring to himself at all.

But then he paused, and really *looked at her*. The air between them stilled. "I don't know, actually," he breathed, "Since I have been like this, I have never tried to touch anyone."

Lisette swallowed and willed her heart to stop hammering like the hooves of one of her uncle's horses on the track. "Would you like to try?"

She knew he was not really breathing, being dead and all, but she swore if he were he was barely doing so now. "Yes, I think I would."

Lisette was frozen in anticipation and something more exciting she did not want to name, but it did not matter as Perry moved first, gliding silently and effortlessly toward her. Their knees were nearly touching, if touch they could, but Lisette was not looking at his knees.

Perry had raised one surprisingly strong and beautifully male hand and was slowly, carefully, reaching out to brush his fingertips to her cheek. Lisette met his eyes but the fire she saw there was too much so with a little sharp little breath she closed them.

How could a man who did not really exist in any meaningful way make her feel like this?

"How does that feel?" Perry asked, his voice hushed and ragged.

"I-" Lisette tried very hard to feel something. "I don't feel anything."

"Nothing at all?"

"No," she said sadly and opened her eyes. His face was mere inches from hers, his form more defined than ever, though she could still make out the flickering firelight on the walls behind him through his beautiful face.

"And this?" He lowered his face to hers fully then and she closed her eyes instinctively to meet the kiss.

It was strange how much it hurt to feel nothing at all.

When she opened her eyes, he had resumed his position next to her before the fire, his form level with the ground now and his eyes still on her.

"That's a damn shame," he said, catching her off guard.

Lisette felt a smile tug at the corners of her mouth. She saw in his eyes that his joking hid the same sadness she felt. "Oh I don't know. Just think, if we had been caught you would have to marry me."

The words were intended as a joke, but he did not so much as smile.

"I should be so lucky," he murmured and if Lisette thought her heart was in the pit of her stomach before it was now somewhere well below her knees.

"Were you-" she asked the question she had been pathetically dreading the answer to for days, "did you ever marry?"

"No."

She felt guilty for the pointless relief that flooded her at the answer, but there it was.

"Did you ever wish to?"

"I knew I had to," Perry said matter-of-factly, "Dukes don't get to decide such things for themselves, they simply are as they are."

"I never thought of it that way. I always thought great power meant greater choices."

"Choice and desire," he said, giving her a look that burned hotter than the coals in the fire before them, "have nothing to do with it. But no, I had not found a bride before I died, if that's what you mean."

Lisette nodded. That was what she meant and words were becoming more difficult to put together. It was getting terribly hot, even though she could hear the cold rain outside rattling on the windows.

Perry went on. "Do you know what has always been the downfall of the men in my family? It was the reason for the curse, and even my death."

Lisette shook her head, unable to take her eyes off him. He was so very handsome, the firelight made him almost look warm and whole and... real.

"It was women."

Lisette returned from her daze enough to narrow her eyes skeptically. "Women?"

"Do not misunderstand me, I adore them. You. All of you," Perry explained, with an encompassing wave of his arms.

"How *did* the curse start, Perry?"

He gave a heavy sigh. "As you say, in for a penny, in for a pound," he muttered half to himself, then began his tale. "My ancestors first came over with the Conquerer, as knights, if the stories are true. They won enough favor and power to be granted a title and, eventually, assumed the duchy of Stafford. It was all very grand- and according to legend, they made the most of it."

"What do you mean? Large houses and piles of gold?"

Perry looked uncomfortable. "Some of that, yes, but they enjoyed their position in more, erm, social ways."

His reticence only increased Lisette's curiosity. "Do you mean whoring?"

Perry choked in surprise. "Language, woman!"

"You don't think ladies know that word?"

"To the contrary, I rather like that you do. I just did not expect it." He met her eyes with a grin.

Lisette drew herself up haughtily. "I am nothing if not surprising."

"Truer words were never spoken," he murmured. "But to continue boring you with my longstanding tales of woe, the men in my family have always had the reputation for being rather.... Wild."

"First, Peregrine, I am the least bored I have ever been in my life. Second, do I want to know what you mean by 'wild'?"

Perry chuckled. "It's nothing terrible. We were not going around murdering people- well, not people we weren't supposed to murder for crown and glory et cetera. No, it is more that the men in my family have always thrown themselves fully into life's delights, shall we say. Without an eye to consequences, or others."

"So whoring?"

"Yes whoring." They were both chuckled at that. It was nice, comfortable, pleasant for all the conversation was bizarre.

"I don't suppose these men in your family also gambled, drank, raced, squabbled and dare I say, caroused?"

"There was carousing, yes. All of the above, ad nauseam."

"That does not sound terribly unusual. Obviously it is not a commendable lifestyle, but there are plenty among us even now who live such lives and enjoy themselves tremendously, or so I am told."

Perry nodded. "It's true these interests are not uncommon, but I am afraid my lineage has always taken them to new heights. Faster horses, more gambling, more winning, certainly more drinking than anyone else, and they loved women so much they ironically treated them as if they did not care at all. They treated everyone as if they did not matter, most especially anyone that did."

"Ah," Lisette said, "I see."

"Yes, I am afraid it was not our wicked behavior that damned us, but our callous hearts."

Lisette looked at him. "But you don't seem to have a callous heart. You are the kindest, most considerate man I have ever met. You have shown me great kindness these last few days. Despite our initial encounter, which was understandable. I would have died if you had not told me where the flint was, let alone the food. You have a better heart than you realize."

"Ah, but my dear, look at me. I do not have a heart at all."

Lisette thought on that a moment, but it was terribly confusing because while he was correct, so was she, and she strongly suspected he was dodging the real topic, anyway.

Confirming her suspicions, he continued with a gruff clearing of his throat, "We have always been, for better or worse, terribly, impressively, unusually selfish. One would imagine we would learn our lessons, but there is something inherent in our male line that just cannot reform, I am afraid. That is why we were cursed."

"Because your ancestor was selfish?"

"To put it simply, yes. He was the eighth Duke of Stafford- I am the fourteenth- and he was by all accounts the worst of the lot. As such, he was immensely popular and very good company- as long as you did not ask him to give anything in return besides, I suppose, a night of wholly incomprehensible pleasure."

"And Anne Boleyn wanted more?"

Perry nodded gravely. "She did. Henry had become tedious, and dear Stafford was anything but that. However, he also refused to be anything more, if you see what I mean. According to the legend she

The Ghost Duke Who Loved Me

left his bed one night to scurry back to her own, unnoticed, but she left behind a golden hair clip. Knowing if it were found she would be ruined and, ironically, executed, and also, according to legend it being her very favorite hairclip, encrusted with four perfect rubies, she returned to claim it."

"Oh dear," Lisette muttered, guessing where the story was going.

"Oh dear, indeed," Perry confirmed. "She had been out of the room but ten minutes and when she opened the door she found dear Stafford carrying on with two of her ladies in waiting and the young man who tended the fires."

"Sounds like he was doing an excellent job," Lisette quipped, "of tending the fires."

Perry laughed that beautiful, full laugh she loved. Loved? Liked. Enjoyed. She enjoyed that he enjoyed her humor and he had a nice laugh, that was all.

Nothing more.

"He certainly was," Perry conceded, still chuckling. "Unfortunately, Anne did not see it that way. To make matters worse, another familial skill, when she entered the room good old Stafford looked up and invited her to jump in and join them. She was furious."

"I imagine so," Lisette mused. This was far more scandalous than anything in even the most outrageous novels.

"She had the ladies in waiting sent to nunneries and the young man locked in the Tower of London, which is rather ironic."

"It is," Lisette agreed, grateful her uncle had allowed her to keep her father's many history books. Anne was a resident of the tower herself before her execution, for, as it were, adultery. "And dear old Stafford got the curse?"

"He did."

The fire flickered ominously and Lisette remembered they were not discussing some mere children's tale, scandalous details aside. The living, or rather, not living, proof of the seriousness of the story was sitting beside her, still faintly translucent in the flickering light.

"What is the curse? Do you know?" Lisette asked, suddenly nervous, even though that was ridiculous. The curse could not hurt her.

Surely.

"I do." He paused. "She had it written down and sent to him on a literal silver platter, sealed with her kiss. The paper was kept through the centuries in a glass case at my ancestral estate. We all grew up

61

knowing it by heart, as if the knowledge of what would come would somehow alter our fate. It's odd though, none of us knew we would become trapped like this as spirits. We always thought it was a curse of death."

"Isn't it?"

"No," Perry said as the light flickered greatly, pushed by an unseen wind. "This space between is far worse."

Lisette swallowed. "So you never met any of your ancestors? You had no idea the curse condemned you to this?"

Perry shook his head. "For all I know I am the only one to suffer this fate. Perchance it condemns others differently, but the words fit. No one realized they were so literal."

"What are the words?"

Perry took a deep breath, then, in a voice deeper and older than any she had yet heard, he uttered:

"As found is found thus bound is bound,
Unto the wicked heartless wound,
Where no thought is given forth
Forever thinking, trapped is worth
After this life before the next
All male souls of the line be hexed
Equal in sin and unknown of love's call
Shall forever be
So binds these words vexed
Trapped in limbo
Never to rest"

At the final word the fire went out, throwing them into total darkness. Lisette cried out, and she felt the weight of something dreadful now in the room with them. Something that made her want to flee. Something hopeless and clawing. The air was the coldest she had ever felt.

A moment later the fire came back, full and blazing as before. Lisette looked at Perry, certain she was nearly as pale as he was.

He looked pleasantly surprised. "Haven't done that in a while, glad to know it still works."

Lisette reached out a hand to hit him playfully on the shoulder, but caught herself just in time. "You tricked me!"

Perry grinned. "No trick. It's the real curse. Obviously."

"But you knew it would it douse the fire and that horrible feeling would come over everything?"

"The fire yes, but what feeling?"

"You did not sense it? That hopelessness and… I don't know, like something terrible was going to happen."

Perry shrugged. "No, but something terrible *has* happened," he gestured at his translucent body, "and I always feel hopeless." He gave her a grin that completely belied his words.

Lisette rolled her eyes. "If the men in your family were half as good company alive as you are dead, I can see why you broke all those hearts."

"We are much better company alive, I promise," he said, heat in his words. Lisette avoided his gaze and cleared her throat.

"So you never saw any other ghosts?"

"No. But I think it may be because all my ancestors died places we never went."

"What do you mean?"

"The original Duke, the eighth Stafford, he died in the middle of a barge party on the Thames. It was while Anne was imprisoned in the Tower, and he thought it would be fun to float by and give her a salute."

Lisette dreaded the answer but knew she had to ask. "How did he die?"

"Struck by lightning just as they passed the Tower. He was drinking out of a golden goblet two feet tall if the stories are correct, while pissing over the side of the boat. He yelled, "Look Anne, I'm a fountain! Make a wish!" and bam, there you have it. Perfectly clear day. Struck dead on the spot."

"The curse is beginning to make more sense."

Perry threw her a rueful smile. "Indeed."

"What about the others?"

"To my knowledge, one died *in* a whorehouse, another *on* a whorehouse- the roof, that is. Two died in duels. And I have a great uncle who died during a bet that he could drink more ale than any man alive in an hour. Depending how you interpret the rules he did, at least, win."

"And what about your father?"

"Ah. That."

The Death

"My father died unexpectedly, as most men in my family do-"

"Then wouldn't the unexpected be expected?" Catching the look in his eye, she added, "I'm sorry!"

"If you don't want to hear the story, I will let you get back to sleep and return to my gothic tomb of an attic."

Lisette clamped her hand over her mouth.

"As I was saying, he died unexpectedly. Even before the curse the, shall we say, *habits* of the Aston men led them to unusual and generally untimely demises, but certainly since the curse these ends became stranger and arrived earlier. Cruelly, each Duke survived just long enough to father a son, meeting his own end shortly afterwards. My father, however, fathered four sons."

"No daughters?"

"None. All boys, all cursed. My father believed more with each subsequent year and each new babe that he had somehow broken the curse, to have lived so long and fathered so many."

"Is that possible?" Lisette could not help but ask *some* questions. "To break the curse?"

"No," Perry said firmly. "It cannot be broken. He did not know, or wish to believe, that, however. It was why my father married my mother. *Her* mother had come from a long line of wise women, practiced in the arcane arts. They were tinkers, Romani, as I said, though her own father, my grandfather, was an Irishman. Poet, I believe."

"That sounds nice."

"It's irrelevant," Perry snapped, and she knew that he did not enjoy this topic. Whether his continuing was due to a wish to appease her or a wish to simply unburden himself, she did not know. Either way, he continued, "My mother had grown up learning the ancient traditions of her mother's people as well as her father's. She came to my paternal grandmother's attention and the family decided it was worth risking the title's reputation to try to bring some new blood into the family line, or at the very least, some new knowledge."

"Did it change anything?"

Perry huffed a bitter laugh. "My mother thought her parents were hawking gibberish. She had seen enough to not believe a word of it. She simply wanted more out of life and saw her chance to be a powerful lady, so she played along when the opportunity arose to be not just any lady, but a duchess. She didn't even believe the curse was real, when he told her."

"But she pretended to?"

"Of course. She instructed him to purchase amulets and scrolls and all manner of bizarre antiquities. The ancestral hall down in Sussex looks like a bloody museum. She loved it all. She had a very curious, scientific mind. Taught herself to read, and read everything she could. The purchases were really all for her own study and gratification, but my father was so desperate to avoid the curse, he was blinded to her true ambitions."

"She was very beautiful as well, was she not? The portrait upstairs is striking."

"She would have been a diamond of the first water, had her breeding allowed it. She knew it, too. She was in so many ways better than my father, but he was so focused on breaking the curse he cared for nothing else, not even his own jewel of a wife. Theirs was not a happy marriage."

"But there were four sons?"

"A child would rather not dwell on such facts about their parents, but for all my own were never friends, they had a genuine physical passion between them. I think both had an inner fire that burned a little too hot."

Lisette nodded, having personally never considered having an inner fire. Passion was as frankly alien to her as curses and dukes. More so, considering she was currently chatting with a duke who was cursed.

"I'm sorry, I'm stalling. All that to say that my father one day received a new treasure, this one from Egypt. I remember when it arrived. It was a golden scarab that fits perfectly in my father's palm with carnelian eyes. It was ancient and beautiful. My mother was very pleased and promised him that based on her research it held hidden properties that would ensure his continued success in fighting the curse."

Foreboding descended on Lisette, but she said nothing.

"We were all standing his study, my two younger brothers by the fireplace, my mother and myself across the desk from him. It took several minutes to open the scarab, which was obviously hollow, a vessel of some sort. Then all at once, he did it."

The feeling of dread wrapped around Lisette like a dark blanket.

"It burst open, the top flying off and tumbling across the desk, the base emitting a cloud of some sort of foul powder the color of swamp water. My mother pulled me back just in time, but the plume enveloped my father and in his shock, he inhaled."

"Oh no," Lisette whispered, the dawning truth worse than she feared.

"He couldn't breathe. His face swelled up, his skin all purple then sort of burning. My mother was screaming, we all of us huddling against the farthest wall of the study, making for the door. Blisters covered his face, his hands, he was crying out in a silent scream as he burned, then my mother pushed us out the door and slammed it shut. A moment later we heard a heavy thud, and that was it."

Lisette was speechless in horror.

Perry shrugged. "I suppose they had their own curses in Egypt. Some are more tangible than others. Obviously the scarab was poisoned. It is a miracle the rest of us made it out of the room alive."

"What- what happened then?"

"Well, back to the important bit, being me, I became the fourteenth Duke of Stafford on the spot. I was nine years old. My mother took us to London that very evening and I never went back to the house. As far as I know they never retrieved my father's body. No one wanted to meet his same end."

"So they just left him there?"

"There were no good options, I'm afraid. The study became his tomb. I considered simply burning the whole place down, but the household staff assured me they had brought a mason in and covered over the whole study outside and in and one need hardly remember it was there at all."

"That's terrible," said Lisette.

"That's life, my dear," he responded ruefully and her heart went out to him.

He gestured to himself, a literal phantom, trapped between this world and the next.

"I am no expert on happiness myself, even though I am afraid my woes cannot hold a candle to that, but I do believe life is not always terrible. Sometimes it is quite wonderful," she added tentatively.

It was Peregrine's turn to look at her with pity. "I have only just begun the story. My mother settled us in London but within a week she had disappeared."

"Disappeared? Was she- taken?"

"If you mean did she take herself away, then yes. She was done with whole mess, and though I do not know if she ever believed in the curse, the manner of my father's death and, if I am generous, perhaps her own guilt over it, was too much for her. She took all her jewelry and disappeared."

"Leaving four young sons?"

"Three. She was pregnant with the fourth, even though she did not know it yet. My brother Heath was delivered on our doorstep five years later with a note written in Italian and a Stafford signet ring. He looked just like the rest of us so we had no doubts he was legitimate."

"You have a very colorful family history."

"Just wait until you hear about my death."

"I *am* waiting," she grinned.

"And you are very patient. I do hope my tales of ancient poisons and magic and foundling children are not too tedious for you?"

"I've heard worse," she said with a sniff, and he chuckled.

"Excellent, because it does not get much better from here, I'm afraid."

"No happily ever afters?"

He did not even smile. "There is no such thing."

Lisette knew better than to point out the bitterness in his tone belied deeper feelings on the matter. Instead, she pivoted. "So what did you do then? When you became Duke?"

"I finished my schooling, then when it came time for a grand tour I took it. Not only did I take it, I added an extra two years, traveling through Arabia and Egypt, even further than that."

Lisette's heart swelled. "You've been to those places?"

Perry shrugged. "I knew the curse would catch up with me, and I wanted to see the world. At least, more of it than just Rome and Venice and Constantinople."

"I would love to see any of those places."

Perry nodded. "There are many wonders in this world. I saw some of them, though in truth everywhere looks the same if you're in a tavern."

"You traveled the world and all you did was drink?"

Perry laughed. "Hardly! I caroused, I seduced, I even got into a few fights. All of which I won, I might add."

The boyish pride was evident, but Lisette felt disappointed. "Did you see the pyramids?"

"Of course. They're hard to miss."

Lisette rolled her eyes. "You know what I mean."

Perry grew somber. "Of course I did. My travels were partly to suck as much out of life as I could, to escape the burden of my past, let alone the responsibilities of being Duke, which I'll admit, I never wanted. I secretly hoped maybe if I went in person there would be some clue, some trail I could find, to break the curse."

"And did you?"

"There was nothing. I never even learned what ancient trickery it was that had killed my father. None of the mages in Egypt had ever heard of such a poison. I returned to England fully convinced there was nothing to be done but accept my fate. And I was right."

Neither of them said anything for a moment. Only the truth of his words and the crackling of the fire echoed between them.

After a moment Lisette asked the question that had haunted her for days. Surely now that he had finally opened up was the time to ask. She hoped she was right. "How exactly did you die? Was it terribly gruesome?"

Perry made a face. "It was not pleasant."

"Peregrine," Lisette asked, really meaning it this time, "how did you die?"

She watched him expectantly, her imagination rapidly conjuring images of stabbings, pistols, and the contraption the French called a guillotine. That last one had not existed in Perry's day, but beheading had, as Anne Boleyn knew all too well.

"My heart failed me."

Lisette blinked. Even her robust imagination had not considered that option. "Do you mean you lost courage a pivotal moment of battle or chival-"

"No. My actual heart just stopped."

"Oh." There had to be more to the story, Lisette was sure of it. She also knew it had to be something truly awful for him to be so reticent to tell her. "How?"

Perry looked like he was preparing to do something particularly unsavory, the sort of thing one absolutely does not wish to do but in a bind one must. He was, as far as Lisette was concerned, in a bind. She had to know.

Looking to the heavens, he sighed the heaviest sigh yet and turned to her. "I was making love to a woman."

Lisette nodded slowly. "And that killed you? That is… surprising, given your age, but one does hear of such things. Certainly in an older man…"

"That's not what did it."

Lisette leaned ever so slightly closer, as if the truth was a hare that would spring away if she could not be near enough to grab it in time.

"She was married, you see," Peregrine continued, looked more pained than ever. "I brought her here while her husband was away."

"Did you love her?" Lisette heard herself ask. The answer hardly mattered, of course. Really, why would she even ask such a thing?

Perry's eyes crinkled at the corners as he chuckled bitterly, shaking his head. "Good god, no. I've never loved anything in my life."

The words landed between them with the telltale thud of truth.

"I am sorry to hear it," Lisette told him, wishing more than ever that she could simply reach out and touch his hand.

He cleared his throat with gruff authority. "Don't be. It's better I avoided all that, with women or family. I think the closest I got was my horse, Jubilee. Terrible name for a stallion, but he was a glorious creature."

Lisette loved horses, but having been raised by an uncle obsessed with them knew that such love was not an adequate substitute for the human kind. "You did not love your parents? Your brothers?"

"My brothers were a royal pain, and I hardly saw them. I was the eldest and educated separately. My father believed he had bucked the curse and I would be the family's salvation. The others were mere spares."

"Is that how you saw them?"

"I hardly saw them at all. I was at my father's side. Always."

Lisette understood then. "Until he died."

"I was arguably at his side, then too," Perry quipped but his voice was hollow. "It was terrible."

"The pain you felt, that was love, Peregrine."

"It was a bloody nuisance," he lashed back, and Lisette knew she had hit a nerve. A deep one. "I never asked to be put on a pedestal, to be separated from my brothers, to be raised, practically alone, by a man so obsessed with his own mortality he never even truly looked at the boy in his shadow. It never occurred to him there are things worse than death."

Lisette said the only thing she could think of. "I'm sorry."

Perry took a steadying breath and raised his hand to his temple. "Don't be, it's all long done and gone. So are they. At any rate, I have never loved a woman, thank god."

There was nothing Lisette found to be thankful for in that fact, but she kept the thought to herself.

"The woman I brought here, I should not have. She cared for me, and I knew it. I also knew her husband was the jealous sort. She was stunning, you see, every man in court was after her, and I was the only she had eyes for."

"Poor you."

"Well, wait until you hear where that got me," Perry said, back to his usual wry demeanor. "They had not been married long, her father had arranged the whole thing. I was so arrogant and naive, I decided now that she was wed I would finally acquiesce to her wishes. I certainly had not offered for her, but I stupidly liked the idea of having her then. After all, I would no longer be forced to marry her if we were caught, she was already married."

"I would think the way it's turned out is considerably worse than being married."

Perry breathed a harsh laugh and grandly gestured to his own transparently otherworldly form. "I don't know, from what I have heard of matrimony this might be a better state."

"You are ridiculous. Continue."

"As my lady desires," Perry said with a roguish wink. Telling the tale of his demise seemed to be less burdensome as he went along. Lisette realized she was the first person to hear the tale aloud, unless he had rehearsed it for some of the mice in the attic.

"The lady in question was only to happy to come away with me here, to the smallest of my hunting lodges and my personal favorite. It's very old you see, and I used to find that charming."

"It is," Lisette said, looking around at the grand old room.

"Spend another eighty years in here and get back to me," Perry said, "The lady at the center of this tale did not share your opinion either, I'm afraid. She wanted ducal grandeur. Her husband was merely a viscount."

"Terrible," Lisette said.

"Indeed. Sadly, *he* was. And in her long-suffering joy of finally being with me, the lady, unbeknownst to me, wrote her husband a letter claiming she was leaving him and was now mine, whatever the law of the land may decree."

"Oh dear."

"Oh dear is right. Her husband broke into the house- that's his handiwork on the kitchen door, if you noticed."

"How could I not? Did he have an ax?"

"Just fists, I believe. He was a very large man, and he was, to his credit, singularly focused. It all would have been quite impressive from his point of view."

"But not, I imagine, from yours."

"No," Perry said drily. "He came upstairs and, having learned which room was mine, beat down the bed chamber door while I was in the middle of, well, you know."

"Enjoying his wife's company?"

"Very much so," Perry nodded and Lisette felt an unbidden and nonsensical rush of envy.

She cleared her throat. "So her husband… he murdered you?"

The grimace returned to Perry's handsome features. "Not exactly."

Lisette was confused. "I don't understand."

"I had been very… *focused*, and, well, the crash of the door and his erm rather aggressive entrance, it, erm…"

Lisette had never seen Perry at a loss for words, and if she did not know better she would swear he was blushing. His cheeks, ever more substantial in the firelight, were a distinctly softer shade of blue.

"It what?"

"It startled me."

Lisette blinked. "Yes, and?"

"That's it."

"What's it?"

"That is how I died."

"You died of… surprise?"

"I believe the clinical term is shock."

Lisette began to giggle. "You were startled to death? Your heart gave out, just like that?"

"I was intensely focused! She was a demanding lover, and once upon a time I had an indomitable will to succeed at everything I bothered to try, particularly if a woman was involved. Anyway, obviously the curse was to blame. I was at the very peak of health. I'm sure if I had had a weak heart I would have known. It's all because I was seducing a married woman I had no intention of doing right by."

He paused thoughtfully. "That, and the decade of heavy drinking, smoking, gambling, whoring, racing, and- well, anyway, some of the other things I had done up to that point. I was no picture of saintly innocence, for all I had witnessed what befell my father."

"I'm sorry but this is too much." Lisette was only half listening. She could not stop laughing. She knew he was self conscious about his death, and that it spoke to greater themes of his virtue and the curse and all that, but shock? Death by surprise? It was the exact opposite of anything she would have expected of him.

"It's just-" she gasped between fits of laughter, "that's- that's how *rabbits* die sometimes, isn't it? Startled to death?"

The stern line of his mouth twitched. "I suppose that's true."

"So you- you-"

He shot her a rueful grin. "Yes. I died like a rabbit."

They both laughed then, the absurdity of it, of him, of them, of all of it, collapsing around them in waves of mirth.

It was the sweetest symphony Lisette had ever heard and she wished it would never end.

The Fire

Perry felt genuine, irrational, wholesome joy coursing through him for the first time he could remember.

He felt free and tightly held at the same time. It was strange and wonderful.

And far too much.

This was bad, very bad.

It needed to end.

Immediately.

Gasping, he caught his breath and stilled himself. It was odd how being dead he could not actually breathe, having no use for it, and yet this damned female left him breathless in ways no bodiless half-life ever could. His initial instinct that she was dangerous had been correct. In fact, he was increasingly suspicious things were far worse than even that- Lisette Havens might prove deadly.

Although deceased nearly a century, the thought chilled him.

She had to go.

It was the only way to ensure his sanity remained intact, and his sanity was all he had. Worse, it was already precarious. He should make her leave now. This very moment. Before everything got worse, because Perry knew, without a doubt, that if she stayed, everything would get worse.

Yes, he would tell her that come dawn she was no longer welcome in his house, and then he would evaporate back to the attic until she left. Or maybe until next month. Or next year, even. Or-

Whenever. It didn't matter. He had all the time in the world. All that mattered was that she leave him alone before she made him feel anything more.

He was a duke, after all. He could make her leave, and he would.

Right.

Now.

Perry opened his mouth, steeling himself to tear her out of his world, like a deeply lodged bullet that must be removed by ones own hand. This particular bullet, he thought dimly, was altogether too close to his heart.

Damn. Stupid thought.

He had no heart.

She had to go.

He took a breath, pointless but steadying, and said the words he needed to say, the words that flayed the corners of his mind begging release, the words that would save him an age of misery. He said...

"You're very beautiful, Lisette."

Bloody hell.

"Oh. Erm, thank you, Perry," she said, her surprise as genuine as its accompanying blush. "I- I don't think anyone has ever said that to me before."

It was his turn to be surprised. All thoughts of removing her from the premises evaporated at the sight of her staring up at him as if he had just uttered the most transcendent poem she had ever heard. "I find that very hard to believe. Impossible, even."

She shook her head and the russet ringlets that framed her delicate face danced in the firelight. She had done no more than brush her hair since her windswept arrival, so he surmised the loosely twisting curls were all her own.

That cascade of copper waves was just as captivating as her personality. *Trouble, trouble, trouble. Send her away.*

"Is something wrong?"

Perry realized he had been staring too intently at a particular strand that twined past her ear into an upturned curl that pointed directly at her perfectly pouted rose pink lips.

"Yes," he said, then caught himself. "I mean- no, nothing is wrong. Lost in thought is all."

Those lips turned up a bit at the corner. "What thoughts could possibly be so distracting, Your Grace?"

If she had not already admitted to her obvious innocence Perry would accuse her of leading him on. However, she could not possibly know what thoughts he was having.

Could she?

"Just thinking about-" Perry's mind raced through its deck of cards, each draw revealing something useless like 'cows' or 'brandy' or 'the cost of shipping from Ceylon,' so finally, he said, "you."

"Me?"

She had spent the last few days believing she was losing her mind, but it was now apparent to Perry that it was he whose mind was well and truly gone. When was the last time, when confronted with a question he did not want to answer, he had told the truth?

"Yes. Your hair."

That was it. He was done for.

Lisette grimaced. "My hair? Whatever for? I know it's a disaster as I haven't been able to pin it at all, but I did try-"

"Hush. I was thinking how perfectly imperfect it is."

She eyed him- justifiably so- with skepticism. "Perfectly imperfect? Is that the way dukes are taught to say 'quite dreadful'?

"On the contrary. I am not sure I have ever seen a lady's coiffure so entirely unmanageable or so wholly enchanting."

"I am still unsure if you are paying me a complement or mocking me, Your Grace. My money is on the latter."

"You told me you don't have any money."

"I don't, but I do have my pride." She raised her chin and looked at him with as much hauteur as any duchess he had ever met. "I do not appreciate mockery. I thought we were having a pleasant evening."

"And so we are," he said, serious again. "I can not recall having ever spent so pleasant an evening."

That caught her off guard. She turned away towards the fire, as if he could miss that blush on her freckle-dusted cheeks.

"Neither can I," he heard her say in a voice that barely reached him over the sounds of crackling flames and ever-howling wind. "You have done more for me than anyone I have ever met, sir. In genuine human kindness and- and showing me there is so much more possibility in life than I had ever dared to imagine."

Her voice was barely above a whisper, and he knew every word cost her, as the truth does when one is accustomed for condemnation when speaking it. For his part, Perry did not think anyone had ever said anything so nice to or about him. That small, dangerous little part deep inside him was hanging on every word. He could not stop it now, nor did he want to, and that was even before she said, in a voice so quiet he had to lean forward to catch each precious syllable, "Is there- is there anything I can do for you, before I go tomorrow?"

Perry froze, unsure if she understood what the husky undertone in those last words meant to him. What it told him she was thinking, whether she knew it herself. He knew it, because he was thinking the same stupid, impossible thing.

"I need nothing, Lisette," he said gruffly, pulling back. "I am nothing."

She spun around, cheeks more flushed than before. "That is not true! You may be little more than a, a floating soul, but there is nothing finer in a man than his soul. You are a greater man without your body, Peregrine Aston, than any man I have ever met who had one. Which is all of them."

The words should have sounded absurd. If anyone overheard them, they would laugh.

Peregrine did not laugh.

He thought it was the finest thing anyone had ever said to him, and even though the girl was wrong and had no idea what a terrible, selfish rake-hell of a man he actually he was, he wanted more than anything for just one moment, this one night, to believe what she said about him was true.

"Close your eyes Lisette," he said, his own voice hoarse with desire. He did not care if she found that offensive. He wanted her and he suspected she wanted him and they would never have each other, but he could give her something to remember him by long after she had left this terrible, cursed place. "There is one thing I want you to do for me."

He watched as her soft green eyes fluttered closed.

"Anything," she said and he had never felt more helpless.

He had never felt helpless at all, come to think of it. This was a first.

It was a terrible feeling.

If only there was something he could do about it...

Then, in a flash of inspiration only a lifetime and then some of studying female pleasure could provide, he had an idea.

"Do you ever touch yourself, Lisette?"

Yet again, Lisette was grateful to already be seated. The flagstones were cold and hard even with her nest of blankets, but they would have been far more so if she had been relying on her knees this evening. Knees that had been little more than untried dough for the last hour.

If his previous compliments had knocked her to the floor, surely this one question would have sent her to the basement.

It was the most embarrassing question anyone had ever asked her.

And the most thrilling.

"Sometimes," she said, surprised at the low, wanting tone of her own voice. It was a voice that belonged to a courtesan, to Cleopatra or Isolde in her bower. It was not a voice that belonged to Lisette Henrietta Havens, definite virgin and burgeoning spinster.

Except it was her voice.

"Will you show me?"

Show him? She could not possibly show him. He was the only person to whom she had ever admitted having any such passions, and she was absolutely not going to elaborate. It was private. Personal. Something for herself alone, and, perhaps one day, the marital bed.

The thought of Ulster appeared unbidden and she blanched.

"You do not have to show me, Lisette, if you do not wish-"

"It's not that! No, I- I was just thinking of the man I am to marry."

It was Perry's turn to pale, if a ghost could do such a thing. It was odd, but Lisette was thinking of him less and less as a spirit, and somehow, he seemed more human ever hour they spent together. He was still transparent but he had more color than before and, were he not made of ethereal vapor, he would now be sitting fully on the floor.

"Is he that bad?" he asked, and it occurred to Lisette that he had been far more forthcoming about his circumstances than she had. It was a jarring realization.

"Worse, by all accounts."

"I feared as much. My offer for you to stay as long as you like still holds," Perry said, and she knew he meant it. "I was so overwhelmed to have a visitor I could tolerate I did not stop to think just what dire straights you are in. Of course, when you first told me it seemed unsavory, but- I sense now it is worse than that. Decades of solitude are my only paltry excuse, and it is a poor one. I am sorry."

He had caught the look on her face. "What is it?"

"You said you can tolerate me," she said mischievously.

He smirked. "Yes, fine praise, I know."

"Indeed. I am honored, Your Grace."

"Do not settle for so little, Lisette," he said and the heat that had briefly vanished returned like a wave crashing over them both. "I can more than tolerate you."

"Don't," she whispered, only half meaning the word.

"Unfortunately, there is little I can do to prove it to you. Perhaps, however, I may guide you?"

"You want me to- to show you?" she said in an even quieter voice, knowing he had not forgotten his earlier question.

Neither had she.

"I want us to explore together. To enjoy what is left of this night. You can show me your pleasures and I might tell you how I should enhance them, if I only had the body to do so."

Lisette could barely breathe. The air in the room was so still, so hot, so overpowering, it was as if time itself had stopped and only the two of them were left alive in the void.

Well, not alive. Conscious.

Trembling with anticipation, Lisette met Peregrine's gaze. "Yes," she said. "Yes, I will show you."

His voice was a low, masculine rumble of desire. "Yes is my favorite word." Lisette could scarcely imagine what it would be like if he had a tangible, physical form. It would be overpowering, this thing between them. Even as he sat there, half translucent in the flicking firelight, eyes burning into her, devouring, she felt they were poised on the edge of a cliff crumbling beneath their feet.

She let herself fall.

Slowly, Lisette leaned back against the blankets surrounding her, letting them slide from her shoulders. Her shift was so old and threadbare she knew it hid nothing, and found for the first time she preferred it that way. She had always felt embarrassed of her poverty, her inexperience, her body, everything, but under the focused beam of Peregrine's heavy, knowing gaze, she felt safe.

She felt wanted.

Her hand moved, slowly, so slowly, to gently pull at the fine fabric at her hip. Up and up it came as she gathered it in her fingers. Peregrine's eyes were riveted to the place she worked, both of them barely breathing, every movement, no matter how slight, rippling through them.

When the linen, nearly as translucent as he was, had pooled around her upper thighs Lisette traced the soft ridges and valley where her leg met her body. The journey took an eternity. The path was soft. When she felt the brush of tight curls, she paused.

"Don't stop," Perry said, sounding like a man lost in the desert who had sighted an oasis on the horizon. "Please don't stop."

The 'please' emboldened her more than anything. She instinctively knew that one single, simple, beautiful word belied his desperation more than any other he, a duke, could utter.

She continued.

Pressing her fingers down lower she felt dampness. It was more moisture than she ever felt when she was alone. She gave a little gasp, both at the realization and at the sensation her own touch shot through her in a blaze of pleasure.

Perry smiled knowingly. "You want me, don't you?"

"Yes," she said with another little gasp, her fingers working slow circles on the nub at the pinnacle of her sex.

"Mmm," he purred, "my favorite word again."

"Do you wish this was your hand, Your Grace?"

"More than anything," he said and she knew it was true. "Perry."

"What?" she paused, dazed.

"Call me Perry. And don't stop, Lisette, please."

That word again. It fell on her ears like sweetest honey.

"What would you do to me if you could, Perry?"

"There are no words for it, or names, at least in this country, for the things I wish I could do to you. And you would enjoy each one more than the last."

Her fingers were moving faster now, and he was hovering closer than ever. His face was mere inches from her own as he leaned over her.

"But I would start," he whispered, "by going a little faster, just there."

She did as he directed and was soon gasping at the edge of that familiar plateau of pleasure which felt wholly new under his riveted gaze.

"Yes, that's it, darling," he breathed, lips inches from her own, but she felt nothing. No soft rush of air. He had no breath.

She faltered at the thought, and he reached out as if to steady her, hold her- he stopped himself.

"What's wrong?"

"It's just- I wish you were alive, Perry. I wish I could touch you."

"Dear God, Lisette, you have no idea how badly I wish the same. Just being here with you these last few days I have felt more alive than I did even before my death."

"Truly?" she breathed, the pleasure growing again.

"Yes."

"That is a wonderful word," she gasped, caught between the sensations building within her and intimacy that was talking to him of such things, "I have noticed you've become more solid the last few days, more real-looking somehow, did you notice?"

He blinked, briefly taken out of the moment. "I have?"

"Yes. Even now, I can barely see through you and you are practically resting on the floor."

He looked down at himself then, as if for the first time in an age. "You're right. I think. I- I really can't say. I never notice any more. I can't feel anything, so I stopped caring- except now, here, with you, I can almost feel it. I can almost feel you, Lisette."

"Pretend, Perry, that you can. And I shall too."

He gave a wicked smirk. "Well I can't feel even my own touch, I'm afraid, otherwise believe me, the afterlife would be far less boring."

Despite the thrums of pleasure pulsing through her, Lisette giggled. "That's very naughty, Your Grace."

"Perry!" he grinned, "And yes, it is. Pity, too. Every man covets the family jewels, don't you know? They must be inspected regularly."

Lisette grinned back. "I wish I could inspect your, your-" A frisson of pleasure shot through her. "Perry!"

"I am your Perry," he said, eyes suddenly serious despite her teasing.

"Yes, you- Oh!" she said, just as the final wave of pleasure broke over her, sudden and overwhelming. A rogue wave, and the only anchor she had to cling to as she was consumed by pleasure's tides was the unwavering hold of Perry's gaze.

"You are magnificent," he breathed as she floated back to the surface. "Lisette, you are-"

"I'm what?" she grinned, now acutely aware that she was sprawled legs akimbo, bared to him, having just revealed her deepest self to this man. This, well, ghost, but when she looked into his eyes, he was all man.

Her man.

The thought was unbidden, and unwanted. He could never be hers, nor she, his. They had only this one night. It had to be enough.

In a few hours, she would be gone.

"What's wrong?" he asked, his hand reaching towards her face as if to move a strand of hair. As always, he caught himself just in time. She wondered what would happen if he *did* touch her.

"I'm tired now. I'm sorry."

He nodded. "Do not apologize, Lisette. Never apologize for telling me what's in your mind. Of course you must be exhausted. I will leave you to sleep." He started to float gently away.

"Perry?"

He turned back to her. "Yes, Lisette?"

"What happens if you kiss me?"

The question caught them both off guard, but as soon as the words left Lisette's lips, she knew she meant them. She needed to know.

"I have no idea," he said sadly.

"Try."

Slowly, Perry floated towards her until he was again only a few inches from her. Lisette sat up straight, heart thumping wildly.

She did not know what she expected, but the thought of making any sort of contact, of feeling him in any way, consumed her like hunger did a starving man. Surely, though she had not felt his touch before, she would feel a kiss?

"Ready?" he asked, his gaze intent.

Lisette nodded.

Her eyelids fluttered down until they were open just enough to make out the lines of his face as it neared hers. She could not feel his breath, but she heard it, ragged as her own. He was as close as he could be.

She closed her eyes completely and waited.

And waited.

And…. waited.

Nothing.

No sensation whatsoever. There was no warmth, no cold, no air or pressure, no moisture, no sense of anything at all.

Her heart sank and she opened her eyes.

Perry was gone.

The Pursuit

The hearth was cold when Lisette awoke hours later. The morning was already advanced and the sun was nearly above the house.

Perry was nowhere to be found.

Lisette wandered the house calling his name, limiting herself to one sweep of each room, all of them dusty and already too familiar to her. She was going to miss this place.

But more importantly, or perhaps simply far worse, she was going to miss its sole occupant.

A sole occupant who obviously did not care a whit about her.

The embarrassment began as a lingering memory on the edges of her consciousness, but it only took half an hour of being awake for it to come crashing down over Lisette. Every empty room, every time she called his name to no response, it became inescapably obvious that Perry was avoiding her. And why not?

What had she been thinking last night?

She had made a fool of herself. That she had not behaved as a lady should was of no consequence- she had no intention of being a 'lady' ever again. She was going to be her own woman from this morning forth, no longer Lisette Havens, but some other, independent being who would be making her own way in the world. *Her* way being the key. The powers of Society said a woman's pleasure was a sinful thing, and while last night might have been the worst mistake of her life, she knew in her very bones it was as far from sinful as one could get.

It had been divine.

The pleasure was not the problem.

Besides, the powers of the world also said there was no such thing as ghosts, and, though the evidence was artfully evading her this morning, she knew that was poppycock, too.

Unfortunately none of these convictions staved off the embarrassment. It was not that she had bared her body to him that troubled her, that he had seen her in the throes of pleasure and known his part in it, the trouble was that she had bared her heart to him. She had never been so free, so vulnerable with anyone, arguably not even herself. He had brought out the truth of her. He had seen the very marrow of her soul. She had displayed her most precious self to, to…

To a man who not only clearly could not care less, but a man who in any functional, real-life, future-looking, life-building way could not care at all.

She was a fool.

Her belongings, including the stash of silver Perry had given her, fit in a single small handbag she had found moldering in an upstairs armoire. It took only a few minutes to gather it all and another minute to reach the front door of the old lodge.

"Goodbye Your Grace!" she called out, willing her voice not to shake or betray the moisture with which her traitorous eyes were threatening her. Then she added, so softly only she and perhaps the nearest stones of the ancient pile could hear, "Goodbye, Perry."

Then Lisette turned on her heel and, with all the righteous confidence of a queen, strode away from the house.

She did not look back.

Perry wanted to die. Ironic, that. Simply turn off the hemorrhaging faucet of feelings that was turning his so-called life upside down and simply be done with it.

He had existed for a long time without a body, surely he did not need thoughts or emotions either.

It was ridiculous. *She* was ridiculous. Preposterous, really. No sensible young woman wandered into a haunted crumbling house and actually *enjoyed* the company of its undead occupant. What had she come here for anyway? He had been perfectly content without her.

A small, annoyingly smug voiced whispered that that was not true, but Perry stifled it.

Miss Lisette Havens had thrown his existence into mayhem but one thing was perfectly clear: he was better off without her.

The path to the main road was overgrown and longer than Lisette had thought, but then her route to the house that first night had been no path at all.

On her way past the old gate, she found a basket of fresh offerings from the village. It weighed her down, but she could hardly decline fresh rolls and roasted chicken. She wondered what frights Perry had subjected the locals to for their fear to tender such scrumptious tribute.

Not that it mattered. They would continue fearing the old house and Perry would continue ensuring their fears were well-founded. It would all happen without Lisette, just as it had for decades.

The road through the woods beyond the gate was really more of a trail. The lodge was not only far from the village, but far even from the main road that led to it. No matter, she had the time, and reliable directions. Perry had given her instructions to reach the road and the village beyond, but from there she was on her own.

For the rest of her life.

At least it would be a life of her own making. She would not be Marchioness of Ulster, that was for certain. Thank god.

What would she be? She had no idea. It would be a difficult road into the unknown, but Lisette knew she would manage.

She had survived living in a haunted house, after all.

In over half an hour of walking Lisette had still not reached the village. She wondered if Perry had been mistaken in his directions. It was possible, after all. He had not gone further than the estate's gate in almost a century.

The road curved just ahead, avoiding an old oak the size of a small house. Lisette slowed, listening.

Voices.

Thank goodness. She was close.

The sooner she found the village and arranged passage on the next mail coach the sooner she would be safely on her way to whatever came next.

She followed the road around the tree with enough hopeful anticipation blossoming in her breast that she could ignore the growing weight in her heart.

Almost.

Perry's face flashed in her mind, and she pushed it away. There was no future there. The sharp pain in her chest that grew with every step she took further away from him would fade into nothing more than gratitude. In many ways he had, with his wisdom and encouragement, given her this new future. The silver didn't hurt, either.

If it were not for him she might well be dead in a ditch in the woods, or worse.

The Ghost Duke Who Loved Me

Passing the oak, Lisette looked into the clearing beyond. The voices were close, surely the village would come into view-

There was no village.

There was only a clearing in which a handful of men sat eating their luncheon in the shadow of a very large, very grand carriage.

"Chit can't 'ave gone far, we'll 'ave 'er by nightfall," one of the men said thickly. His mouth was full, but that had not stopped his conversation.

"If she's even alive," another man said darkly.

All the men laughed.

Lisette did not see the humor in their words. In fact, with a growing sense of horror, she saw a future that was suddenly very, very bad.

"Stop your jabbering and get me another pasty!" a loud voice commanded from the carriage just as a thick, puffy hand on the end of a thick, puffy arm jutted out from the conveyance's window.

One of the men scrambled to deliver the requested pasty.

The sense of horror grew as Lissette looked again at the carriage, focusing on the ornately carved door.

The letter "U" with a badger on one side and a gourd on the other.

Ulster had come for her.

Lisette had to get out of here. She took a step back on instinct, and, stepping on her skirts, tumbled to the ground.

Ulster's men looked up.

"Oy! You there-"

"It's the chit!"

Pandemonium erupted. All four men were scrambling to put down their lunch, gather their weapons, and tell Ulster they had found her. The result was a lot of indistinct shouting, but in the midst of it, the smallest and quickest of the men made straight for her.

Lisette scrambled backwards, but she did not made it far before her back was against the ancient oak.

"Don't be afraid, gel," the man said, revealing dark brown teeth, "his lordship has found ye. Yer safe now."

"I'm not going with you! I- I'm not who you're looking for. I'm from the village."

The man tutted with a grim look. "Yer a pretty thing, don't spoil yerself with lies. His lordship don't like lies."

"I'm not lying!" she cried, her voice shrill in her own ears.

"Well that makes two in a row," he said, and Lisette could see the others finally making their way to join him. There was something very

85

familiar about the gang, but she couldn't place what as she was distracted by the unfolding vision behind them. The carriage rocked ominously until the outline of a very large, unkempt old man was visible craning out from the tiny window.

"Two lies is too many," the small man laughed at his own humor. The others, not knowing the joke, laughed anyway. "No more, gel."

The man lunged for her, but Lisette was ready. A long silver serving knife drove home into the man's thigh just as his hands clutched at her. He recoiled, howling in pain. His comrades, obviously not as intelligent as their injured companion, all stopped to ogle him as he writhed.

In a flash, she knew who they were. These were the same highwaymen who had waylaid her carriage. Was Ulster hiring them out to rob local travelers? No wonder the man was rich as Croesus.

A shout brought her back to the moment.

"Don't stop you fools! Get her!" Ulster called from the carriage, which rattled alarmingly as he attempted to exit it without their assistance.

Lisette barely noticed, however. She was already on her feet, and by the time the three other men came after her, she was already running far ahead.

Perry moved the white bishop three spaces diagonally, taking the black pawn.

Or he would have, if he could maneuver physical objects according to his will with that level of precision. Sometimes he could, but it wholly unreliable and made him devilish tired to try, so he didn't use the skill for chess. Pity. All these years and he still had not figured out how to maximize his potential as a spirit of the netherworld.

Instead he stared at his chessboard, pieces frozen in a game that had been interrupted eighty-two years ago, and ran the moves in his mind. He had been practicing this way for decades now and could keep an entire game's worth of moves on both sides in his mind, more or less.

As he was only playing himself the occasional cheating never raised any hackles.

This time, as a matter of fact, it appeared white would win.

Pity, he always preferred black.

Maybe if he went back a bit and let that knight-

A horrendous crash like a herd of elephants breaking down the walls came from below stairs.

"Damn squirrels probably got in, knocking over that statue of William the old-"

Perry stilled. He could hear a voice, faint and ragged, calling his name. Or gasping it, more like. The voice sounded terrible, and he realized with a start, familiar

Praying that his mind was merely playing tricks on him, he moved towards the source of the voice. It was coming from the entry hall, just as it had a few days- was it only a few days?- ago.

"Lisette?" he called out, reaching the dimly lit entry. The sky had been been building to rain all day and now the clouds were dark as dusk. Perry had no idea what time it actually was, but it did not matter- whatever the hour, she should not be here.

Yet as he looked at the floor in front of the ancient oak door, there she was, crumpled on her knees and breathing as if she had just run for her very life.

"You're back," he said, dumbfounded. God he wished he could touch her, just to know she was real. Just… because. "What's wrong?"

"They're coming," she gasped, looking up at him, sweat-soaked hair loose and clinging to her bright red cheeks. "They're coming for me."

"Who is coming for you? What are you talking about?"

"Ulster," she said, and Perry felt a loud roar in his ears. He felt the sensation of his fists clenching.

"That bastard," Perry cursed, wishing there was something he could hit, something like Ulster's ruddy, bulbous face, "He can't have you."

Lisette shook her head. He had never seen fear in her eyes until now. He did not like it. It went poorly with the colors of fresh spring grass and notes of intelligence and joy that usually resided there. He would not allow this. He would not let Ulster have her.

"It's too late. My uncle signed the papers. As far as he's concerned, I am his."

"No, Lisette, you are mine."

Lisette thought running at breakneck speed through the woods, dodging tree branches and brambles in an effort to avoid the obvious line of the road had taken her breath away.

She was wrong.

Perry's words did.

"Yours?"

"Yes, by god or whatever damned power has brought me here, yes, Lisette. You are mine, and I will not let him take you."

Their eyes met, more passion and fire than Lisette had ever felt, coursing between them. It was nearly a tangible thing. Lisette could feel the very stuff that made the stars and sea swirling around them, holding them, confirming the truth of his words. Of course. They belonged together.

Then a flicker of sadness flashed across his beautiful face and he turned away. This would have been the perfect moment to draw their bodies together, to kiss as if it would be their last- which it could.

Except they could not kiss. They could not embrace. That one earth-shattering look was all they could ever have, fate be damned. Lisette was cursed now, too, in a different way, and she would have the rest of her dreary mortal life to dwell on it.

But now was not a time for dwelling, it was a time for action.

"He has four men with him," Lisette said, rising shakily to her feet. She had fallen several times in the woods and while she could still move about she knew she would pay for it later. "Four men and a carriage. At least two of the men were on my heels to the edge of the grounds. I do not know where they are now."

Perry nodded, all duke. "Go to the kitchens, that is the easiest place to fortify. There is a storage closet there across from the hearth, hide yourself there."

"And what will you do?" she asked.

"I have my ways," he said with a wicked grin that made him look like a naughty schoolboy. "You don't think I deterred every man or woman who came near this place in the last century with just some barbed insults and ducal glares, do you?"

Despite the situation, Lisette giggled. "No. I suspect you are far more capable than the average duke of striking fear in the local townspeople."

"That, my dear, is an understatement."

Lisette took a step towards the kitchens, then paused, thinking. "Should I help you before I go? Barricade a door or something?"

"No, no need. We will hear them coming long before they get here, I know this place better than I know my own-"

At that moment the ancient oak door collapsed inwards, crashing onto the floor of the entryway in a billowing cloud of dust. She leapt backwards just in time to miss the massive slab that cracked the floorboards where it landed.

She looked back to where Perry had just been, but he was gone. Her stomach dropped. What if the darkness she had seen in the attic took him over again? He couldn't control it- what if he couldn't help her after all?

It appeared she was on her own.

Steeling herself, she turned to face the yawning emptiness of the doorframe.

Through the dust, shapes emerged.

"Well, well, well, poppet, of all my wives, you certainly have the most spirit already."

The Stranger

Lisette watched in rising horror as the dust settled, revealing a mountain of a man in the doorway.

Ulster.

The four henchman flanked him, two holding the heavy log they had used to batter down the door. The other two, including the one she had stabbed, who was limping badly, stepped into the house.

Ulster, leaning heavily on an ornately carved cane, followed.

He was massive in every way. So tall his head nearly brushed the top of the doorframe and so wide the same was true of the sides, he looked the very opposite of health. His sparse white hair was overlong and knotted, clinging to the sweaty sheen of his mottled, red face. He had the skin and nose of a heavy drinker and even from across the hall Lisette could smell the mixture of brandy, sweat, and rot that came from him.

She wanted to retch.

Instead, she stood tall, chin high, for all the world as regal as the duchess she would never be.

"Spirit?" she asked with the single quirk of her brow that had always enraged her uncle. "What a keen observation. I do have spirit, Ulster. You would be shocked to learned just how much."

The old man laughed. It sounded like old boulders crumbling. "I assure you, my dear, I am very much looking forward to the education."

Lisette smiled back blandly, mind racing. Where was Perry? He had disappeared when she needed him most. Again. If it was the Darkness-

Ulster smiled back. "That's a good chit. Let's make quick work of it and get in the carriage now, eh?" He was missing at least three teeth and the rest looked like the bottom of a pond.

"I appreciate the invitation, my lord, but I'm afraid I must decline." Lisette stalled. She had to do something. She had to escape. They were too close, though, there was not enough space or time. She looked around for a weapon. She felt for her knife in her boot, but it was gone, fallen in her flight.

Ulster caught the direction of her thoughts. "Pity, that," he smirked, all cat to her mouse. "No antique armor for you here, gel. And no need to use that filthy little blade you already showed us. If you come easy, it'll go easy. I have no desire to take home damaged goods."

"Excellent, then let's agree to ensure you don't and I shan't go with you at all."

Ulster laughed again and Lisette tried to keep the fear down. *Where was Perry?*

"Afraid not. Better you come a little roughed up than not at all," Ulster said, as if they were discussing the condition of her henhouse back home, or the weather. Then his grin turned dark, and Lisette could see the fate that awaited her. Perry had been right. There were things worse than death. "Get her, boys."

At the words, the henchman, all four of whom were now inside, flanking Ulster at the door, lunged forward.

And all hell broke loose.

All light in the already dim hall went out, though no candles had been lit and it was, as far as Lisette knew, the middle of the afternoon. They were plunged into blackness.

"What the-" she heard one of Ulster's men say, but the rest of his words were lost in the sudden wind that swept through the room.

Perry.

If Lisette had thought her first night had been frightening it was nothing compared to this. The wind tore through the room. It shrieked as if with the sound of a thousand voices, tortured, screaming, as the air whipped and swirled around them. Lisette fought to remain standing.

The men were all shouting but no words could cut through the tempest. Bits of wood and plaster were flying off the walls, and Lisette watched as an entire chair was carried up, up, up nearly to the chandelier, where it hung, twirling in midair.

There was just enough light to make out the shadowed forms of the men. For now they were distracted, but she knew the effect would not last long.

Lisette ducked down onto her knees and crawled along the wall towards her bag, which lay cast aside halfway to the door.

She had nearly reached it when Ulster spotted her. "Get her! Forget this witchcraft, grab the girl! Meet me in the coach!"

Unfortunately his words reached the men despite the howling wind. They all turned to her at once and stumbled against the force of the maelstrom towards her.

One, bearded and tall, reached her first. Lisette tried to pull back, but she was against the wall. He lunged and she felt his callused hands close around her ankle. He pulled.

Lisette screamed as she was dragged across the floor. The man laughed, revealing he, too had been raised with minimal appreciation of dental care. This fact made Lisette feel better when the heel of her other boot made contact with his jaw with a horrible crunch.

Howling in pain, he let go. Just in time, as another of the men, the oldest and most grizzled of the four, reached out for her.

Before he made contact, however, the chair came crashing down from above right onto the man's head. He crumpled, landing beside Lisette. She saw the lines of a long, thin dagger in his belt. She grabbed it before he could stop her and stood, back to the wall, facing the men.

Bits of debris were still flying about, the wind stronger than ever. It was impossible now to hear anything. She felt as if they were in the middle of a hurricane, and though she knew it was all to protect her, she also knew there was a power in Perry he could not control. The Darkness beyond his humanity that not even he could trust.

She needed to get out here. It was the only way to ensure her safety. Even a week in the woods alone would be worth it if she knew she would be free. There were too many men to take down even with whatever help Perry could provide. The wind was distracting, but already the men were becoming accustomed to it. Perry could only do so much.

Then, part of the ceiling caved in.

"Watch out!" the bearded man cried. But it was too late. The fourth and youngest of the lot- that same young man who had ridden in the carriage was it only a few nights ago?- had been struck by a massive beam. Light shone through where a gaping hole now opened into the attic. A beam from the very top of the house had splinted and crashed all the way down onto the lifeless form of the young man.

Lisette gasped in horror. Watching the other three take in this development and turn on her with greater fury in their eyes, Lisette knew violence would be the only way.

The Ghost Duke Who Loved Me

The wind pushed them back and pressed Lisette against the wall, the force of it unreal. Then it assumed a voice, far darker and more terrible than any Lisette had heard on that first night. The agony in it sent a chill straight through her.

"GETTT OUTTTTTT!!!" it cried, sounding nothing like the Perry she knew. It did not sound human at all.

She should listen to it, as much as the men. If she could just cross to the other side of the room, where the hallway narrowed and led to the kitchen, she could go out the back and lose herself in the woods while they were distracted.

Except, they were not distracted.

The untimely loss of their companion seemed only to strengthen the resolve of the other three- as the oldest one had gotten up from under the remains of the chair- to take Lisette and be done with it. Even the ever-strengthening wind was losing any power over them.

All three were fixed on her, calculating their next move. She raised the dagger in her hand until it glimmered in front of her. Even in the midst of the chaos there was no mistaking their intention, or hers. They wanted her, and she would not be taken.

With a yell all three ran at her at once.

Lisette slashed her blade through the air before her just as a crack lightning blinded them all and the house shook with the single loudest shot of thunder she had ever heard.

Suddenly, they were not alone. As the wind ravaged the room around them, a ghostly pale figure, all frayed and eery white light roughly in the form of a man, darted amongst them. As the ringing of the thunder in her ears subsided, Lisette could hear the figure laughing in the jagged darkness.

The effect was terrifying. And thrilling.

Perry was toying with the men now, who had realized they were dealing with something more than a freak trick of the weather.

"The Devil is here lads!" one of them shouted, his words shredded by the wind.

Perry was appearing in front of one, then disappearing just as soon as the man reached for him. The small man with the wounded leg had his own dagger out and was slashing at Perry whenever he appeared before him, but the blade had no effect. Of course it didn't. Perry had no body.

The dead duke himself merely laughed, the sound eerily clear in the midst of the storm.

Lisette watched as he led the three men, who were wholly focused now on the unearthly threat in their midst, on a sort of dance.

He would appear before one, then suddenly behind another, until they were all circling each other, unaware of their comrades, each focused only on the specter eluding them. Toying with them.

Finally, in a deft and Lisette realized wholly intentional move, Perry appeared before one. "Boo!" he said drily and spun to the left. The man, seeing no humor in the situation, spun to follow and only stopped when his blade had lodged in the side of one of his companions.

Both men shouted, the one with the knife protruding from his side markedly louder than the other, who had released his hold on the blade.

Perry laughed louder than ever then evaporated.

"That's it," the small man growled. "Enough! 'E's playing us for fools, lads."

"Look at me!" the one with the knife in his side said. It was the older man. The wound was obviously not an immediately a mortal one, as the man had ample padding to keep the blade from any essential parts.

The bearded man grasped the handle and ripped it straight out. The older one howled in pain.

"Tighten yer belt on it. Let's git the gel, and git out of here. I'm done with with this devilry!" he shouted against the still roiling wind.

In all the chaos Lisette had quite forgotten her own role in the action. She should have fled for the kitchen ages ago, but she had been mesmerized by Perry's skilled choreography.

Stupid, she chided herself. *Now what?*

Perry seemed to have the same thought, as he had reappeared, making himself more solid now, less ephemeral. He was floating behind the men, who had returned their attention to Lisette.

He gave Lisette a wink.

"Surround 'er, lads. She won't escape this time."

The need for instructions confirmed Lisette's working theory that the small man was the only one with any brains. That was probably for the best, though given all three were much larger than she was it hardly helped in the face of their approach. One wrapped around the hall on either side, and the bearded one came at her straight on.

Still floating above and behind them, unnoticed, Perry cleared his throat. The whipping wind, which had not let up, allowed this small sound to reach them all quite clearly.

The men paused and turned around.

"Apologies, gentlemen, I have been remiss. Before you go I must introduce you to my friends," he said as though they were all afternoon callers at the end of a tea service.

Lisette's brow furrowed in confusion. Perry had no friends. The thought did not stop her, however, as the moment the men turned their backs she began to slink along the back of the room, past the stairs, in the direction of the kitchen.

"I don't care about yer friends, demon," the small man sneered. "Ye may make a mess and mischief, but yer kind can't touch us as is flesh and bone."

"Ah," Perry said with a polite bow of his head, "but I am afraid you cannot say the same for my friends."

No sooner had the words left his lips than a new sound, like a herd of wild horses pummeling towards them, rumbled from the very walls of the house.

Before Lisette could do more than pull herself up to perch on the curved end of the bannister- the stairs being as far as she had gotten- the room was crawling in rats.

Rats were running down the stairs. Rats were coming up out of loose floorboards. Rats ran in front of the open frame where the front door had been and even out from behind the portraits on the walls were they had obviously carved doorways of their own.

Lisette did not know Perry could summon animals to his beck and call but then there were so many things did not know about him. Their gazes met above the pandemonium and she smiled.

He smiled back, and gave her another wink.

God, she loved this man.

Oh God- she realized with the greatest horror she had felt all week, which was saying something- *she loved Perry*.

The revelation was profoundly inconvenient, distinctly futile, and wholly, inescapably, true. She loved him.

She loved a duke, which was surprising and impossible enough, but even worse, she loved a ghost. A wicked, mischievous, clever, powerful, enchanting ghost that made her feel more alive than anyone else she had ever known.

And just now that ghost was saving her life.

Between Perry and the rats, the three remaining men were fighting for their own lives. Perry was knocking objects at them with such random force Lisette did not know if it was intentional or not. Either way, she thought, as she watched an old all clock smash into the bearded man's head, it was working.

So were the rats. They were clawing and biting, crawling up clothes and pulling at the men's hair.

If she could only manage to cross the stairs and get to the kitchen hallway without the rats mistaking her for one of their targets-

Thoughts of escape were cut short however by the unmistakable sound of a gunshot.

The small man had pulled out a pistol and was shooting at the rats, which were scratching and snapping and attempting to overwhelm him and his two fellows. The pistol did little to deter them. For every one rat the man hit, three more took its place, and he could not very well aim at his own legs or his friends.

Then, a look of triumph on his face, he pointed the pistol at Lisette.

"Call 'em off!" he roared, "Or the gel gets it! Ulster can find another bloody cunt fer a wife!"

As if someone had snuffed a candle, everything stopped. The howling wind ceased. Bits of debris caught mid-air fell to the floor. The rats stopped their onslaught, disappearing in moments back to their dark corners.

The only sound left was the heavy breathing of the small man and the whimpering of his two fellows. And the thudding of Lisette's heart.

"Put down the pistol," Perry said calmly, every inch a duke again.

"I'm no fool. The moment I do, ye'll set it off again."

"You have my word, I shall not," Perry said, avoiding Lisette's gaze. It had never occurred to her how unnerving it was to have a pistol pointed pointed at one, aimed to kill.

If only she had made it to the other bannister, she could make a run for it-

"Eh, I don't put much store by a dead man's word," the small man said cruelly. "Think I'm better off doing it my way. Don't like takin' chances, see? Better off nice and clean and done wiv it."

The crack of gunshot shattered the quiet air. Lisette heard herself breathe in sharply, a gasp she did not finish. It was as if time slowed and she could see the bullet cleaving the air between the barrel of the pistol and her breast. There was nothing to be done about it. She had always been quick on her feet, but she was not fast enough for this. No one was.

So she sat, frozen on the bannister, like the hopeless, useless creature her uncle had always accused her of being.

"No good will come of you," he used to say.

And he was right.

That, of all things in this moment between moments, bothered her most.

No good had come of her, and now, it never would.

Oh well.

Then, suddenly, miraculous, she was not alone.

Perry was there, in front of her. Floating, between her and the bullet, as if that would do anything.

He had certainly grown less translucent, more substantial, since she had first arrived, but it as all illusion. There was nothing to him but ether and light. He could do nothing to stop the bullet.

She wished she had time to tell him thank you, anyway.

To tell him that she would have done the same for him.

To tell him that she loved him.

Her gasp reformed itself, coalescing into an exhale, into words, into-

"Perry I love you!" she cried out, certain this was all happening too fast for any of it to matter.

He did not turn around. He did not even try to respond. How could he?

The bullet hit him, shooting shreds of ghostly light in it's path. Lisette could see the bullet as it moved through him, its route undeterred, its destination her heart.

There was something deeply romantic, she decided, about dying like this.

Maybe the two of them could haunt the old lodge together now. Surely no one would dare bother them after the damage this afternoon had done. The place was a wreck. It was perfect. They could be together forever.

Except, something was wrong.

The bullet had stopped. Midway through Perry's chest, it had simply stopped, trapped inside him like an insect in amber.

He turned to her then and opened his mouth, his eyes radiant with shock and pain and something that looked very much like love. "I-" he mouthed.

But the rest of his words were lost. From the center of him, the bullet began to melt, which made Perry himself start to melt. He began to evaporate, shedding strands and bits of light, right in front of her.

His eyes were last to fade, locked on hers, frozen in a last, lingering, heart-shattering look.

There was a blinding flash of white, and Lisette blinked. When she opened her eyes, he was gone.

She slid to the floor and wept.

It took only a few moments for Ulster's men to gather themselves. They were shaken, but they were too well trained in Ulster's bidding to fail, especially when they had conquered the apparent resistance.

Ulster was not a patient man, after all, and he had been waiting in his carriage too long already.

The small man and the bearded one pulled the body of their fellow out from under the rubble as the oldest man stepped forward, admittedly gingerly, to gather Lisette in his arms.

She did not resist at all.

Why would she?

Her life was over. It did not matter what Ulster did to her. It did not even matter if he died on their wedding night and left her a fortune.

She had no use for fortunes. Or husbands.

She thought she had only wanted her freedom, but now she saw it meant nothing without Perry.

Shaking uncontrollably, she let the darkness that reached out take her, with arms far more overpowering than those of the man who carried her, limping and weak, towards the door.

"I don't know who raised you, gentlemen, but it's not polite to leave without saying goodbye," a voice said from somewhere behind her. The words made no sense, but the voice sounded familiar.

Too familiar.

Impossibly familiar.

A heavy thud told her the other two men had dropped the body they had been holding. The one who carried her slowly turned and then he dropped her, too.

She landed painfully on the floor in the middle of the hall, but she did not care. She was already following their shocked gazes to the top of the stairs.

Perry stood there.

Which was impossible.

But that was not all.

She gasped, loud and full this time.

"Don't worry, darling," Perry said. "We'll have the place to ourselves again in no time."

"You're- alive?" she finally managed.

"It seems I am."

The Duke

Lisette was dreaming. It was the only explanation. Somewhere in the melee she had been hit over the head and was now lying unconscious, her body prone and her mind, well, standing in the midst of the broken house gawking at the man on the stairs.

Because there was no mistake- he was a *man*.

A living, breathing, devastatingly handsome *man*.

"Now gentlemen," Perry returned his attention to Ulster's henchmen, who were watching gobstruck. "As I was saying, it's in very poor taste to not say farewell. It's even worse to overstay your welcome."

"Witchcraft," one of the men whispered, fear palpable in his shaking voice.

"Hardly," Perry quipped. "It's a simple of upbringing. Yours, I'm sorry to say, was clearly lacking."

He was alive. He was *here*. He had a *body*. Her mind couldn't make sense of it.

"This is impossible," she said. For the second time in her life, Lisette thought she might faint.

It appeared two of Ulster's henchmen felt the same way. The smallest man, however, was made of sterner stuff. He turned to Lisette with a bitter laugh. "What, thought yer devil lover abandoned you?" he sneered. "With skirts as light as yers, gel, I wouldna blame ye. Or 'im."

"What did you say?" Perry asked quietly, brushing invisible dust off his sleeve. The words cracked through the room like a whip. No one moved.

The henchman, oblivious to the nervous glances the other two men exchanged, drew himself up. "I said I wouldn't blame ye fer leavin' 'er.

100

Never mind this black magick, any chit acts like a whore deserves to be treated like a-"

However the man intended to finish his statement Lisette would never know, because Perry had, in a single catlike leap, landed at the foot of the stairs and plunged a long, elegant blade into the man's heart.

The man crumpled to the floor, and Perry removed his blade. Looking up at the other three, he gave a rueful smile. "Anyone share his opinion?"

"You bastard," the man closest to Perry growled. "You killed him!"

"There are worse fates," Perry replied. "At least he earned his."

With an enraged yell, both remaining men charged Perry at once.

Lisette scrambled to her feet, her jaw remaining on the floor. She had never seen anything like this.

Perry ducked and whirled, thrust and leapt. He moved like a big cat or maybe a dancer. Somehow, inexplicably, both. It was beautiful and terrible and Lisette could not tear her eyes away. It was poetry in motion, swirling assurance and grace, and entirely dangerous. He moved like the very angel of death himself.

Lisette knew this was her chance. She needed to get out of the house and hide. Perry would find her, and perhaps if she were gone, it would be easier for him to finish the business.

She took a step but a large, meaty hand stayed her.

"Not so fast," a voice hissed on a breath that smelled of onions and far worse. Ulster. Lisette recoiled from his grasp but his other hand came up to hold her fast.

For a man of such obvious infirmity he was surprisingly strong. He was also deceptively quick. The cane abandoned, and Lisette now suspected largely for show, Ulster dragged her backwards towards the doorway and the waiting carriage beyond.

"Perry!" she shouted, and immediately regretted it.

He turned, his one moment of weakness giving the bearded man's blade a chance to slice his arm. Perry shouted once in pain then turned and fully decked the man so hard his nose broke instantly. He fell to the ground unconscious and bleeding.

That still left the older man, however, and Lisette was now almost to the door. She struggled like a wildcat, making it difficult for Ulster despite his size and strength to keep a hold of her.

As he stepped onto the gravel outside and pulled her through the doorframe she managed to sink her teeth into his right hand. The taste of blood nearly made her retch but she did not release him.

Unfortunately, he did not release her, either.

Then Perry's words from last night- was it only last night?- reached her. *Every man covets the family jewels.*

Lisette pushed herself forward as far as she could, then with all the force she could manage, she flung herself backwards.

Her hair pin, useful for the first time in days, struck home.

Ulster released her immediately and fell to the ground in agony, the sharp bronze implement stuck in his crotch like blade. Her hair, ever resistant to being tamed, freed itself easily as she leaned forward.

She staggered up, breathing hard, but triumphant.

Until a strong arm wrapped once again around her waist.

Lisette jumped and slammed her fists in the broad chest of her captor.

"Easy! Easy!" Perry cried. "It's just me, love. It's only me."

Lisette stilled and turned to look up at him. He, too, was breathing hard, and something in his eyes told her it was not just from the exertion of battle.

She glanced over his shoulder. Four bodies lay motionless amidst the debris on the hall floor.

"You made quick work of that," she said drily.

Perry grinned. "I could say the same to you. Not much to look at, is he?"

They both looked down at Ulster, who lay on the dirt clutching himself and moaning.

"Not really, no," she said.

"Sure you want to marry him?"

"On second thought, I think I would rather not. Do you think we can arrange that?"

"Let's ask," Perry said, stepping forward and tapping the toe of one booted foot against Ulster's heaving form. "My lord?"

"What the bloody devil do you want," Ulster ground out.

"Miss Havens would like to extricate herself from your matrimonial arrangement. Do you find yourself agreeable to the suggestion?"

"Go to hell," Ulster spat.

"I've already been," Perry returned, and, pulling out the small man's pistol, shot Ulster once, precisely where the hair pin protruded.

Ulster howled.

Perry turned back to Lisette, who was watching, eyes wide.

"Thought I would finish the job you so rightly began," he said lightly.

"While I don't generally approve of violence, Your Grace, I think you may have just done the marriageable women of England a great service."

"I try," he said.

It was grim work getting Ulster and his men back into their carriage, but they did, driving the equipage to the main road and pointing it in the direction of the village. Lisette gave the lead horse a thanks and a good swat and watched as the carriage rattled into the darkening woods, Ulster's moans echoing into the dusk. It was nearly nightfall.

Finally, standing side by side at the ruined old gate, they were alone. A tremor of nerves ran through Lisette, which was silly, given all they had been through. But then, everything was different now.

She turned towards Perry, feeling like a nervous schoolgirl.

"You're back," she said.

"I had unfinished business." His voice was molten velvet.

"You did? I mean, you do?"

"Mhmm," he nodded, the dim light under the ancient trees doing nothing to diminish how very real he was now, or how handsome. "I was about to tell the woman I love something important and I was interrupted, you see."

It took a moment for the words to sink in. "The woman you-"

"Love. Yes. You see, it's very important, what I meant to say to her."

Lisette looked down and realized she was clinging to him. How had that happened? Oh well. He smelled of pine needles and old books. "What did you want to say to this woman you love?"

"I wanted to *tell* her that I love her. She did not know, you see. I didn't know either, really, until that very moment, when she said she loved me. She said it first, and I have to say it back. You understand?"

"Perfectly. I suppose since the moment has passed you should tell her as soon as possible."

"I believe you are right," Perry said, one hand curling around her waist and the other barely touching her chin, raising her face to meet his under the light of the rising moon. "I love you, Lisette. I love you."

He kissed her then, and though it was their first kiss, it felt like they had done this a thousand times before, in every age, in every form.

The world was full of mysteries, and while Lisette knew she did not have all the answers, she had the one answer she needed.

"If you keep kissing me like that, Your Grace, I would say you have a great deal of unfinished business."

Perry laughed then, the sound at once familiar and foreign, the vitality of life ringing through him in a way it had not before. Fully of hope, joy, love, and the promise of something Lisette had not dared let herself dream of- a future, together.

"What do you say we go back inside and finish some of this business you speak of?"

"I say yes, Your Grace, a thousand times, yes."

He gave her a smile that would have devastated Anne Boleyn herself and purred, "My favorite word."

In short order they were curled before the inglenook. The fire was blazing and for the first time since he could remember Perry was grateful for its warmth. He could *feel* warmth. It was a revelation.

But it paled in comparison to the way Lisette felt, pressed against him, as he ravished her mouth with every kiss he had been unable to give her since the moment they met.

"How?" she asked sometime later, looking up at him tousled and dazed, which was exactly how he felt.

"How what?" he asked, his mind having wandered off in bliss some time before.

"How are you real?"

"You know, I ask myself the same thing about you," he quipped.

She swatted him playfully. "It's not funny. I feel I'm losing my mind all over again. How is it you came back to life? I saw you disappear."

Perry shrugged. "I honestly don't know. Maybe we'll never know."

"Never is long time."

"You would be surprised how quickly time moves once you've had enough of it," he said, burying his face in her hair. She smelled of vanilla and lavender and the combination was even more potent than he had imagined. All of her was more than he had imagined.

Watching her last night- dear god was it only last night?- was one thing, but actually touching her, feeling her, smelling her, tasting her, dear god, that was another.

"You were magnificent today," she purred into his chest hair. Sometime in the last hour his shirt had come off. The realization only made it more infuriating that she was still wearing her shift.

"You want to see magnificent?" he asked, unable to help himself. Reaching over to the threadbare neckline of the linen shift that had tortured him for the last week, he grasped hold of the fabric and neatly ripped it in two.

Her gasp was just as satisfying as the view that was revealed. "There, my dear, is magnificence," he said, gesturing to her soft, flushed figure bared before him.

"You are very, very wicked," she said, making no effort to cover herself.

"I am only just beginning," he returned, and leaned down to follow through with his threat.

Lisette felt she had now died and gone to heaven. Not to make light of what Perry had been through, but she could think of nothing more divine than the feel of him, all of him, against her, kissing, licking, caressing.

When finally neither of them could stand it a moment longer, he finally entered her. The sensation, at first a sharp pain, was quickly overwhelmed with ecstasy.

She knew intellectually what happened between a man and a woman, and had managed to read a few naughty novels one of the more unconventional matrons at church had once lent her in secret, but nothing she had read or heard or imagined compared to what it was like to make love with Peregrine Aston.

They fit together like two halves of a Grecian urn separated long ago and brought back together, timeless, perfect, only for each other.

Perhaps Grecian urns were an odd comparison, Lisette thought fleetingly between gasps of pure pleasure, but then, why not? She suspected she could sit and think for a century and not come up with adequate words to describe what was passing between them.

Perry pushed into her slowly at first, kissing her neck, nibbling her ear, burying his head in her hair like she was his very salvation. His weight upon her was a blessing, his every move a revelation. It took a few moments but soon she had figured out how to move, to match his rhythm with her own, meet it, challenge it, share it.

She had never felt so wholly seen or so wholly loved.

Looking in her eyes as he gave first one deep thrust and then another, she saw the truth in his steady gaze. He felt the same.

"I love you, Peregrine," she sighed.

"And I love you," he returned, pairing the words with a brush of his thumb in the place where their bodies joined. The contact sent all thoughts, of love, of him, of Grecian urns, of the King himself and anything at all, out of Lisette's mind.

She cried out in pleasure, and he matched it, groaning as they raced, together, for some destination Lisette could not see or find on her own.

But she was not worried, she knew he would get her there. In fact, they would reach it together.

And they did.

The End

Epilogue

Two years later

Perry still had to pinch himself. No longer every day, but most days. After nearly a century of nothing changing, now it felt as if every day were a different lifetime. In some ways, it was.

The mystery of how he had come back to life remained officially unsolved, as, he suspected, it always would. One could certainly not go to the nearest vicar or university professor and ask them for answers as to how one was left undead for the better part of a century only to suddenly regain a body and a whole new chance at life, now could they?

Perry's best guess- and this was the leading theory in Lisette's mind as well- was that when he had jumped in front of her to take the bullet meant for her himself, it had broken the curse. The men in his line had been so blindly selfish for so long none of them had ever figured it out. It made sense, he supposed, as much as the thought of any curse made any sense in the first place.

Ah well. There was a great deal of mystery in life, and he had had enough of it to last him a lifetime. Now, he did not ask too many questions, he simply took each day as it came, grateful and, for the first time in his life, humble.

It was a novel experience.

These days everything in his life was a novel experience.

He had a wife, a comfortable home by the sea with what might well be the most beautiful rose garden in England, a steady income of well-placed investments funded by the sale of all marketable items from the old lodge, and, any minute now, a babe.

Truly, he marveled at the magnificence of it all.

"Milord, it's nearly time," the midwife said, peaking her capped head out through the bedroom door. From the chamber beyond Perry heard the unmistakable sounds of severe pain, and as much as he hated to see Lisette suffer, he knew she could handle it. She could handle anything, his Lisette. She was the bravest person he knew.

"I'll be right there," he assured the nurse. It was highly unusual for a father to witness the actual birth of his child, but Perry had seen so very much of death that he rather thrilled to the idea of watching life itself. The beginning, fresh, pure, untouched potential and wholly unconditional love.

He was ecstatic. He would make it all up to Lisette, too, as soon as she was able- and interested. He would do anything for her, and well she knew it.

Ah well, he had spent so much of his energy giving nothing meaningful to women or anyone else, it was high time he paid them all back. Or, at least, a few of them. His family.

He had not had a family in so long he had mostly forgotten what it was like. Not that it mattered much, this new family of his would be quite different than anything he had been raised with, or Lisette either, for that matter. They were not their forebears.

Thank God.

The nurse's head appeared again.

"Now, m'lord!"

Perry rose, butterflies the size of sparrows dancing in his belly. He had not been nervous in a very long time.

It was uncomfortable, but exciting, like many of the best things in life.

With a steadying breath, Perry opened the bedchamber door and, head held high, walked eagerly into his future.

A Message From The Author

Dear Reader,

I hope you enjoyed reading Lisette and Peregrine's tale half as much as I enjoyed writing it. I have always adored old school romances fraught with gothic tension, memorable scenery, a strong-willed heroine and, of course, an undeniably sexy hero. If you have found these elements in *The Ghost Duke Who Loved Me* my work is done!

. . . or is it? There are three more stories in the Dearly Departed Dukes series. You didn't think I would ignore Perry's equally sexy (and equally ghostly) brothers, did you? They too have that woe-begotten, admittedly well-earned, and undeniably fateful family curse to contend with... not to mention three more well-matched, fiercely lovely, strong-willed women who must suddenly face the fact that ghosts are surprisingly real... and surprisingly irresistible.

If you enjoyed this book please consider leaving a rating and review. It makes a world of difference to a self-published author such as myself, and also gives me the opportunity to know what you liked, what you didn't, and what else perhaps you would enjoy in future works. Romance is not an island, after all. (But if you want it to be, I suppose that could be quite fun, couldn't it? Robinson Crusoe shirtless on the beach and all that.)

Thank you for meeting the first Ghost Duke, I hope he lived- pun very much intended- up to your expectations.

If not, he's got three brothers.

Lucky you.

Sincerely,
Cynthia Hunt

* * *

P.S. - If you want to stay up to date on all my forthcoming releases, news of my doings, and freebies (!) please follow my author page on Amazon, find me on Facebook or Instagram @cynthiahuntromance, or, yes, even TikTok @cynthiahunt.romance

Manufactured by Amazon.ca
Bolton, ON